Erik, my love,

Defeating The Moose
Laura Bilodeau

Thank you for you undying support. I love to love you! ♡

♡ Laura Bilodeau

Copyright © 2024 by Laura Bilodeau

All rights reserved.

No part of this publication may be reproduced, distributed, or transmitted in any form or by any means, including photocopying, recording, or other electronic or mechanical methods, without the prior written permission of the publisher, except as permitted by U.S. copyright law.

The story, all names, characters, and incidents portrayed in this production are fictitious. No identification with actual persons (living or deceased), places, buildings, and products is intended or should be inferred.

Book Cover by Laura Bilodeau

Edited and Formatted by Jason Nickey

First edition 2024

This book is dedicated to every cretinous waste of air and space who puts drugs into hands they don't belong. Who rip innocent families apart. Who ruin lives knowingly. To big pharma and all of the crooked doctors and pharmacists. To all the abusive piece of shit men (and women) who make their partner's lives absolute torture. I hope you have the day you deserve. With all the disrespect in the world,

Fuck You, eat shit.

Note to the Reader

Dear Reader,

If you're reading this, it means I've made it. I've made it here, to tell my story. Though this story is fiction, it is based loosely on a lot of things I went through firsthand that shaped me into the person writing this today, your author. I made it, I've got my two beautiful boys asleep beside me, safe, fed and happy who I owe the world and more. This book has a lot of triggers, hell it was incredibly triggering for me just to write. But revenge is a dish best served cold and this is a big fat fuck you to a time in my life I'm ready to close the chapters on and the cathartic release this book has given me, for all the revenge I couldn't seek for legal, and moral reasons. I hope you enjoy this book. There will be no happy ending to this story, that's mine to revel in, for making it here. Not every story needs a happy ending to serve its purpose. If you or someone you know is struggling with abuse in any form, be it physical, emotional, sexual, substance or otherwise, please seek the help you deserve. Don't ignore it and become a crotchety old hag like me. You matter. We made it.

Contents

1. Wake Up Call — 1
2. The Stomp — 7
3. The Meetup — 19
4. Bella Luna — 27
5. Endless Cycles — 37
6. Marcus the Accordion — 45
7. Beer, Cashews, and Blood — 53
8. "Birthdays Were the Worst Days" — 61
9. Definitely NOT a Set-up — 71
10. The Meetup Pt. 2 — 81
11. Revenge Rendezvous Pt. 1 — 87
12. Revenge Rendezvous Pt. 2 — 93
13. "What a Weird Day" — 99

14.	A First for Everything	105
15.	BREAKING NEWS	117
16.	It Was Me	123
Epilogue		133
Special Thanks		135
About the author		137

Chapter 1
Wake Up Call

"Wake your ass up!"

I heard the disgruntled voice shred through my semi-awakened state, and just as my eyes fluttered open, that's when the thick crack met my face with just as much heat as there was sting.

"What the hell was that for? It's hardly 5am." I winced rubbing my now throbbing right cheek. The sting was now a burn spreading across my face like a wildfire that dared not be tamed. I'd become used to this; though there was a half functional alarm clock just inches from my head, the shouts and blows dealt by Marcus at all hours of the day were a much more effective way to wake me. I asked once more, the anger brewing inside of me, "MARCUS, what the *fuck* was that for? It is five in the goddamn morni..."

"THWACK!"

Before I could finish the sentence, I was silenced by yet another blow, this one knocking me nearly unconscious as my head slammed into the wall. A part of me wished I'd passed out, at least then I might get a few more moments of peace and quiet.

"Quit running that pretty little mouth of yours, Doll. You know those dick suckers could be put to much better use than bitching about what time it is. We need to be ready for D, if he ever fucking answers me. His useless ass skimped me or something and now I'm all out. Now wake the fuck up and suck my dick or shut up and do something useful for a change and find me my lighter. And not the red one. You know that's bad luck."

'D'; the single letter I despised most out of all 26 in the alphabet. David was one of the two brothers Marcus dealt with most when re-upping his supply. He and his brother, Stuart, known on the block as 'Mayhem', were good-for-nothing scoundrels who slipped under the police's radar for far too long, whether by luck, ignorance, or force I don't know. Maybe a combination of all three kept them running these streets, but I couldn't wait for the day I'd watch it all crumble and burn before me.

I looked over at the broken alarm clock again, trying to convince myself what I was seeing wasn't true. The green LED numbers fading on the cracked screen read 4:57. There was no chance in hell David would answer any time soon. I swung one leg over the side of the bed, then groaned as my second foot found its place on the ground beside it. The bruises scattering my legs were still sore and forming from the night before. I mustered up the strength and minimal willpower to stand myself upright, but just as quickly lost all motivation. I was running solely in survival mode at this point.

"Hurry up, Doll. You're burning daylight when I want to be burning this spoon. Shit, I've got like 2 good hits left on this fucking thing and I'll be damned if I waste them."

Those words were the driving force to set me forward, both in search of this godforsaken lighter, and to appease this man in hopes he will pipe down for five minutes while I get my bearings.

Miserable prick, I thought to myself.

I shuffled through my bag, knowing damn well he had a perfectly good lighter somewhere within arm's reach. He was just too damn lazy to find it himself. His one-track mind focused solely on his next high at all times these days, it wasn't always like this though.

"Here," I grunted as I hucked the black mini BIC across the bed to where Marcus sat hunched over. I used a little more force than was needed, but hey, can you blame me?

I knew he wouldn't complain. I'd already pried off the metal safety mechanism the day before, making it easier to flick. They called them crack lighters around here, and that's just the way he liked it. I turned on my heels as the sounds of clanking metal filled the cold and dusty room, my cue that the coast was clear, for now, and I made my way to the kitchen.

The familiar rumble and hiss stirred me from my daze as the smell of coffee invaded my nose, a welcome sign that the Keurig had finished, and I could start the second cup. I knew Marcus would have a tizzy if I made myself one and not him. I added the Starbucks Cinnamon Dolce Latte creamer to both cups and stirred them generously before returning to the dungeon I had just receded from minutes prior.

I breeched the doorway and was met with a sight I was no stranger to.

"Yeah, just two hits right?"

DEFEATING THE MOOSE

The words spat out like venom on my tongue as I slapped Marcus across the face. I wasn't dealing with another overdose today. Luckily, or maybe not so luckily for me, the smack was enough to pull him out of his trance. He untied my pink phone charger from around his bicep, his recent tourniquet of choice, and removed the needle from his arm before wrapping the rest of his supplies back up in the tattered facecloth and tucked them back between the wall and the mattress that lie on the floor.

"Sorry," he mumbled as he shifted his weight back onto the bed, "and thanks, for the coffee... You always make it just right, Doll."

He finished the coffee in one swig before rolling over and falling asleep, clearly forgetting his whole tirade about David, and needing to be ready to meet him as soon as he'd answered. A sigh of relief escaped me. I knew I had a few hours before the chaos erupted again.

Looking over at Marcus sleeping was a mix of emotions. I was glad to be in the eye of the storm, but just looking at him made me feel violently ill. The six-foot-four behemoth of a man, who when sober was as meek as a mouse, lay there basically lifeless. His clothes were worn and tattered. When was the last time he allowed me to wash them? At this point, they probably could have stood up on their own. The scent that emanated from his pores was a mix of sweat, grime, shit and God knows what else.

He was worse for wear these days and it was a damn shame. He used to be such a sight for sore eyes. It was like God had handcrafted him special, cut him from a different cloth. His sockets were filled with eyes that better resembled marbles, big and bright, the bluest blue you could have ever dreamed. His skin was soft and even, his hair flowed aimlessly to the side. He was beautiful. That was the Marcus I knew. This Marcus, replaced by whoever this skeleton of a man that slumped before me was, left me feeling like I was living with a complete stranger.

They called him 'Moose' on the streets, for whatever reason, I was not akin to it. If you asked me, it was because if you looked at him now, he resembled nothing more than a tall, lanky doofus that bobbed his head around and was clumsy and combative. Better off left alone in the wild, far away from any human interactions. I wish it were that way at least.

Chapter 2
The Stomp

5 years earlier...

"What are you wearing tonight? Have you heard from Danika yet?" Lynn shouted from the bathroom in our small apartment.

"Marie should be home soon, then we can head out. Look hot, we're finding you a man tonight, Bells."

I continued shuffling through my closet, nothing seeming good enough for this night. After three eighty-hour work weeks in a row I desperately needed a night on the town. When Nikki offered to cover my shift tonight at the pub, I wasn't going to pass her up. I made a mental note to thank her next time we saw each other.

"Bells! Did you hear anything I said? Have you talked to Danika yet? Is she working tonight?" Lynn huffed at me, the toothbrush still in her hand as she barged into my crowded room.

"Huh? Yes, sorry. Just trying to find an outfit. I'll text her."

I grabbed my phone off the charger and plopped on my bed as I swiped up on the screen. A quick smile crossed my face when I saw the background photo was changed to one of Lynn, Marie and I on New Years Eve a few months ago. One of them must've changed it while I was sleeping. We were as thick as thieves, there were no secrets and they had full access to my phone and socials, as did I, theirs.

Danika is the regular Friday bartender down at The Stomp, our local country dive bar. It's a popular little place, with good food, pool tables, a nice floor for line dancing and overall, a good atmosphere without too much hassle a majority of the time. It was our typical stomping ground when we'd go out, so it was only natural that we'd go there tonight. We hadn't talked in weeks since the last time I went out and she'd messaged to make sure we'd made it back home safe.

"Hey hot stuff, are you working tonight?"

Before I could click my phone to off "BabyDan" popped across the notification bar showing she'd already replied.

"Of course! Do I get to see your fine ass tonight? It's been five-ever. XO"

"Dan's working tonight, I'll be ready soon! Are we getting food first, or just eating there?"

"Wherever the wind blows us, Bells. It's girl's night out!"

I slipped into my tightest fitting ripped blue jeans and a coral slouch top that showed just enough of my curves without openly begging for attention. My boots, admittedly a bit rough around the edges, sat by my door, but that's to be expected after years of shuffling across that wooden dance floor down at The Stomp. I used to get out and dance much more, but these days the only do-si-do I was performing was around the three other bars I manned across the city. I slipped the boots on and skipped over to the bathroom, hoping Lynn would be finished so I could start beating my face and conceal these designer bags that had taken up residency under my eyes. As I rounded the corner, Marie was stumbling through our front foyer looking as frazzled as ever.

"Girl what happened to you, rather... *who* happened to you? Was it Jay? I keep telling you, you can't get over him if you keep getting under him, but you do you, boo-boo!" I shot her a reassuring smile.

I watched as I continued to the bathroom, laughing to myself as she rushed to drop her bags and keys on the counter so she could go fix whatever rat had nested in her hair, and makeup smudged across her face.

"Boo, you whore, it wasn't Jay. Don't worry about me, worry about the cobwebs between your legs. Come on, it's been what, two years since you left Ben? Get a grip. Go get plowed, then we will talk."

Instant laughter erupted from both the kitchen and Lynn's room with that remark. I can't say I didn't chuckle myself, but she wasn't wrong. I'd given up all hope after Ben and I'd split, but tonight, I was determined to change that.

The late spring breeze circled around us, finally warm enough to ride with the windows down. We decided to ride together in Marie's 2008 Ford Taurus. It was a hoopty, and had a wobbly bumper, but Shelby got us from point A to point B and wasn't distracting enough for someone to want to break into. She was a trusty ole' girl, and we had many memories with her. How the name Shelby came about, I'm not sure. We were leaving Target one day and Lynn called the car "Shelby". It stuck.

DEFEATING THE MOOSE

The sounds of Luke Combs blasted through the radio. If you thought Marie couldn't turn the speakers any louder, you thought wrong. We belted the lyrics to 'One Number Away' as we pulled into The Stomp. It was ten of eight, and the regular crowds would be rolling in soon; the perfect chance for us to get inside and secure a table and order some food before then. Tables were hard to come by on Friday nights, so it was by pure luck we got there just in time to snag the last open high top.

As the girls settled in, I scurried over to where Danika was already hard at work prepping the night's garnishes. She finished polishing the last bottle on the rail and looked up just in time to see me hurrying over.

"There's my girl! How are you, babes. New man yet? Pfft, who am I kidding? I haven't seen you bring a man around these parts in ages. Change that soon, why don't you? Now get over here and give me some sugar!"

Danika's bright pink hair fell halfway down her back and blazed as bright as a unicorn that had caught fire along a sunset sky somewhere. She smelled overwhelmingly like cherry blossoms and a hint of cherry vodka; clearly a quick start to her night before her shift began, letting the edge off just enough. I pulled her into a tight squeeze, letting her plump tits suffocate me. She was taller than me, and I nuzzled perfectly between her jugs. She knew I was straight, but I sure was a sucker for those hugs. I'd make a point to get at least one more to hold me over before the night ended.

"Danika, don't be foolish. You know I'll never find a man. I work way too much and I'm too busy loving on you in my free time. I'll take a Sex on the Beach in lieu of a man though, and 2 long islands for Lynn and Marie. You can start me a tab. Have a good night, hun. I'll be back around to visit."

I made my way back to the corner table and placed the three drinks down just as our waitress was coming by with an order of Ronny's cheese curds. She knew we'd order them to snack on while we decided on our meals, so it was convenient that they came out quick and left us no time to wait in between.

"Thanks Beck" we all said in unison.

"You bet girlies. Gimme a nod when you're ready to order. I'll be around in a jiff!"

Beck was an old timer at the bar, but she was a sweetheart. She was in her mid-fifties with a heart of gold and a soul that was a hundred years old. She'd adopted many of us as extended children over the years. You know the type. We all love her. No one dared cross Beck, not in this bar, not in this lifetime. Their heads would be out on a line before the next song could play.

We hardly needed menus, but for old times' sake, we flipped through them aimlessly anyways as we all agreed on our own meals. A chef salad for Lynn, a bacon cheeseburger for Marie, and hot wings for me. We all knew I could use a little more spice in my boring life. Within fifteen minutes of small talk and killing time, our drinks were empty but the plates in front of us were overflowing. Ronny, the head line-chef, had the hots for Marie. Who didn't? - and he always made sure to take care of us when it came to our orders.

Small towns were good for that, and ours was exceptional. We took care of our own and kept the outsiders at bay for the most part. We were defensive to a fault and didn't give many second chances. Loyalty ran deep in the heart of the quiet corner. That's the nickname for the northeastern corner of Connecticut where we called home. The girls always bugged me to find work closer to home. I worked in Worcester; it was only about a half hour up the highway into Massachusetts but the work was better out there. The city had more to offer me when it came to employment, but you wouldn't catch me dead kicking back in any of the three bars I worked in. I was a firm believer that you don't shit where you eat, and I stuck to that.

The DJ for the night began playing the normal country playlist that would get people on the floor, and it worked, as soon as Tracy Byrd's 'Watermelon Crawl' came over the speakers I was practically jumping out of my seat to make my way to the floor. After 3 more dances back-to-back I receded to the bar for a second round from the lovely Miss Danika.

"Thanks snookums" I said in the most playful flirty voice as she scotched the drink my way.

"It's on me" she said with a wink!

"I owe ya, Dan."

As luck would have it, there in the dark back corner of the room stood my demise. Tall, broody, handsome, and full of mystery. A real suburban cowboy Casanova if I'd ever seen one. An air of curiosity enveloped me, but it was too soon to act on my thoughts, curiosity killed the cat after all.

It was nearing 11:30, the drinks had been flowing strong all night, the mystery man kept his sights on me the entire night as I spun carelessly around the floor, Marie and Lynn seemed to notice too.

"You'd be a fool not to notice lamb chop over there drooling over you the last 2 hours. Shoot your shot or I'll shoot it for you."

Marie was the pushy type, but fate must've sided with her today. He was closing the distance between us, and fast.

I had just enough time to give a quick "don't try me" glance to the girls and smooth my hair before his hands landed on our table.

"Seems like a real dishonor for a group of girls like you to *not* be accompanied by a guy like me. But if you girls don't mind, the DJ just put on a perfect shadow dance, and I'll be stealing your little doll here for that."

All it took was one look from his crystal blue eyes and I knew there was no saying "no" to him, not tonight, not ever if I had any say in the matter. Before I knew it, I was shadowing his motions, perfectly in sync with all the other couples outlining the floor, as Luke Bryan's 'I Don't Want This Night to End' boomed through the speakers. The song faded into the next and his eyes said enough for me to know, my night may not have started with him but it sure as hell was ending with him.

After a few more dances wrapped around his finger and being dipped lower than I have ever been before, mostly everyone was clearing out of the bar. The girls hadn't taken their watchful eyes off of me, nor had Danika. I needed one last smoosh of her big, now inevitably sweaty tits and I would be ready to close my tab and head out with my girls. I just had to find a way to say goodnight to ... shit, I never even got his name! I could feel my cheeks redden at that thought, I just danced with this guy for hours and I couldn't even have the courtesy to find out his name? Way to go Arabella.

"Hey babe, the girls and I are going to head out, you can run my card to close the tab!"

My voice was hoarse from all the laughing I didn't even notice I'd done and having to shout over the music to have any audible conversations.

"Add a bottle of water to that too, please, my love."

Danika shot me a wink before running my card. She grabbed a Smart Water from the staff cooler and slid me the bottle, card and receipt. The total was at least 3 drinks short from what I expected it to be, but that's just how Danika was, and Lord help me if I tried to fight her for it. I'd just make up for it with my tip. I dropped a 50 on the bar top and slid it her way, promptly turning to walk away before she could protest.

It caught my eye before I even had a chance to react, the man of my night, standing at the table with Marie and Lynn, great what were they filling his head with. I put a little pep in my step, ramping up the casual stroll I had previously been committed to. I wasn't even back to my table before I was hoisted over his shoulder in a fireman carry as he stalked towards the back door.

"Where are we going? I have to get home! I don't even know your name" I giggled as I playfully pounded on his back.

"Leave the worrying and questions to me. It's Marcus. Your friends said you don't have work until 4 tomorrow. You'll make it there, but for tonight, you're coming with me. Stop squirming before I give you a real reason to."

Whew! A bad boy with a purpose. This side of him didn't show all night. This was probably going to be against my better judgment. I knew I should've protested and made sure I got home. but none of that mattered while I was literally helplessly careened over Marcus's broad shoulders.

Within two months I was packing my boxes to move in with him, the rest... was history, including my friendships with Danika, Marie and Lynn.

Chapter 3
The Meetup

The sun rays cascaded across the ceiling in the dusty trailer bedroom, creating a makeshift galaxy with all the dust particles in the air. Turning to my side, I craned my neck to check the time. 9:28! I nearly jumped out of my skin, but relief washed over me as I realized Marcus was still stuck in his drug induced stupor. Good. No shot I was going to poke the bear. The longer he slept and left me the fuck alone, the better. Maybe I could actually get an uninterrupted shower and some personal hygiene in, it had been weeks since I last shaved, and properly caring for my hair or skin was about as prominent a thought in my mind as brussels sprouts. It wasn't.

I opened Spotify on my phone and let the DJ choose my music for me.

"What's up, I'm your DJ 'X', how about some music you had in rotation a few years ago."

I rolled my eyes but welcomed the nostalgia as I allowed myself to miss my friends. Nostalgia quickly turned into anger and resentment though. What was meant to be a 'self-care shower' turned into forty minutes of rage and my tears going one for one with the water.

"Wasted on You" by Casadee Pope played and it was done for me after that, I needed a way out of this hell that kept me prisoner day in and day out.

You might be asking yourself, "Arabella, why don't you just leave?" Well, lucky you, you likely have never been in a situation like mine. Hostage to a man who has entire control over who you are, every aspect of who you can be, every minute of every miserable day. Financial control, mental control, physical control, sexual control; you name it - he had it. When you've seen the things I've seen, *done* the things I've done, been to the places I've been, endured the pain I've endured, and lost everything that has ever meant ANYTHING to you, then you'll understand why leaving is not an option. Marcus simply would NOT allow that, under any circumstances, at least not alive.

By the grace of only God himself, whatever, or whomever God might be at this point, I managed to finish my shower still unscathed and no sign of life from the bedroom as of yet. I gripped the water handle shaking as I aimed it down and let the water drip off me before stepping out onto the stained and musty towel, a makeshift bathmat that had replaced the actual bathmat that Marcus had vomited all over three months ago.

Getting a new one was definitely not in the budget, according to him. It was a luxury we just didn't need. In his eyes, *everything* was a goddamn luxury it seems. We lived off frozenmicrowave meals, leftover takeout, coffee, and water. On occasion, when Marcus would go on an extraordinarily long bender, he'd come home with extra beer and I could steal one or two without him noticing, but that was mighty infrequent.

I slipped on my bathrobe that hung on the back of the bathroom door, one of the few nice things that had survived the last few years with me. It had become a comfort item for me because of that. Not much was constant in my life anymore outside of the chaos, but that robe was always available to wrap around me and cloak me in an imaginary world of safety and serenity.

I tiptoed to the room as carefully as humanly possible and slipped back onto my side of the bed so I wouldn't disturb Marcus. His phone lit up "D". I had half a thought to open his phone and delete the message. Before the thought could even process through my mind as right or wrong, the beast had awakened.

" Touch it and it'll be the last thing you do."

Marcus swatted his hand down in search of the shattered iPhone. He patted a few times before clutching his meaty fingers around it.

"7 missed messages and 3 calls. Jesus Arabella what the FUCK are you good for? Where the fuck were you, getting railed on the back deck? Fucking whore."

Shit, D must have called while I was in the shower and I missed it, not that that's my problem anyway. I wouldn't have answered either way. No other thoughts could even enter or exit my mind space before the back of Marcus's hand was laying a kiss across my cheek.

"Don't bother asking what the *FUCK* that one was for. You can think about it. Matter of fact, let me help you out, you're clearly too fucking ignorant to think for yourself. When my phone rings, you tell me. When a text comes in, you tell me. When you're going to ignore me to go be the neighborhood cum slut, YOU TELL ME. You hear me, bitch?"

"Charming, thank you master. Harder next time, please." I sneered through clenched teeth against better judgment.

I could usually bite my tongue and control my mouth, but days like today, it was going to get me in trouble. I'd just have to deal with that as it happened. Regardless, it must've struck him enough because his only reply to that was a grunt and an eye roll. A win in my book.

"Get ready, we're leaving in five. He wants to meet over at the old bowling alley. He said he had other shit to do in that area and to meet him there in 20. Do NOT make me late."

I slipped into my shoes and hoodie trying to cover as many marks and bruises as possible, not that it mattered, but it was embarrassing to be seen in public like that. Especially in a town like this, everyone knew me. Talk is cheap and everyone had two cents to throw in. Out the door we went, less than five minutes later.

"Lookin' good, Doll. Hop in. I'll drive today. You just rest your pretty little self in that seat and don't you worry 'bout a thing. Daddy Marcus gotchu girl."

I could've puked. How cringy could he get? He was seriously a sour patch kid; how could he go from smacking me around to sweet-talking me in a matter of minutes?

It was only a matter of silent minutes before we were pulling into the parking lot to the abandoned bowling alley. I used to come down here with Lynn and Marie a lot on nights we didn't intend to drink. The dilapidated building was hardly standing anymore, all of it's windows and doors were boarded up with no trespass signs littering the walls. From the far end of the parking lot you could hear YNW Melly's 'Murder on my Mind' nearing closer, I didn't even have to glance back to know the source of the sound, D was here.

"What's good, Moose?" D said with his suave demeanor, like he wasn't doing a literal drug deal in broad daylight.

He was about as average as they come. 5 foot 10, average build, not too thin, not too thick. A gunslinging Goldilocks of sorts. The only big thing about him were his ego and his passive aggressive attitude. The chip on his shoulder was damn near rotten, however. His hair was a dusty blonde and from the look on his face there was nothing but a box of rocks rattling around inside his head.

Shocker. He was a multi-purpose drug dealer to be fair. I swear all addicts and dealers shared that same pathetic look.

"What's good D? Sorry brotha, this little doll over here thought I needed some beauty sleep. I missed your calls."

That's when a side we'd never seen of D came out. He leaned right in the drivers' side window. Nearly nose to nose with Marcus, he lowered his eyes and bared his teeth with a clenched jaw. The veins in his neck were bulging and his brows were furrowed, never once breaking eye contact, you could practically cut through the tension with a spoon.

"*THIS* is your last dose from me. Do not ever contact me again. I don't know where you get off thinking you can threaten *me* when your useless fucking ass relies on me every single day. Motherfucker, I OWN you, Moose. Calling me all hours of the day asking for a front, selling dumb shit every chance you get; you are fucking pathetic. Take this and get the fuck out of here. Good luck finding more because the boys and I are done. Start treating your girl right before one of us fuck her so good she'll forget you ever existed. We all see the shit you put her through, the bruises she tries to cover, how she cowers in her seat.

We see it all dipshit. You're not fucking slick. I hope you fucking d-"

He was cut off abruptly as Marcus's fingers wrapped around his neck, the awkward angle making it difficult to accomplish anything more than pissing D off further. Just as I went to intervene, D aimed his head back and blew a sickening blow across the dead center of Marcus's face. One headbutt and the whole interaction was over. Marcus was temporarily knocked unconscious as blood began to squirt from his nose, splattering the steering wheel and windshield before him. D shot me a quick wink as he turned and walked away like nothing had ever happened.

Marcus would never hear from D again.

Chapter 4
Bella Luna

4 years earlier...

"Baby! Are you almost ready, sweet stuff? Our reservation is in an hour and it's still a 20-minute ride."

It was Marcus and I's first anniversary and he had planned a whole surprise dinner for us somewhere fancy. I have a few suspicions but nothing for certain. Hopefully somewhere Italian though. I'm really craving some bread rolls.

I took one last look in the mirror, the tight, red, satin dress sat midway up my thigh, the slit in the left side rose even higher, nearly to my hip, leaving little to the imagination. The bodice was lined with rhinestones and had one thick strap that went over my right shoulder to hold it in place. It was the perfect dress, it hugged my curves just right, pushing my mediocre tits up making them strikingly larger to the unassuming eye, I slipped a white cardigan over my shoulders that was nearly as long as the dress itself, grabbed my clutch purse and strapped on my sandals. It was mid September, so it was still just warm enough for sandals but not an occasion that really warranted me wearing high heels, I wasn't *that* fancy. A quick barrage of spritzes from my Victoria's Secret perfume and I was out the bedroom door in no time, my stomach already beginning to grumble with impatience.

I approached the stairs and began to descend, Marcus glanced at me and appeared somewhat like a star struck teenager outside of a Justin Bieber concert in 2008 and a deer in headlights. It was equally dopey and cute, but he needed to snap out our it if we were going to make it out the door instead of to the couch. He had on a plain black T-shirt, his favorite faded blue Levi jeans and crisp, white Jordans. He too spritzed himself with some Polo cologne and we were ready to go.

The moon was just making its appearance for the night as the pinks and oranges painted the sky, something that could never cease to amaze me. Marcus probably got annoyed by how often I would point out the beauty and wonder of the sky at any given point of the day, it didn't matter, dusk, dawn, stormy sky or otherwise, there was always something that caught my attention which seemed worthy of sharing.

"Look babe! It's Orion's Belt. It's so beautiful, it's my favorite constellation to find!"

"It might be beautiful, Doll, but nothing and no one will ever be as beautiful as you. Happy anniversary, my love." He pulled my hand in and planted a kiss on my palm then placed it on my cheek as we carried on down the highway towards the restaurant Marcus still withheld from me.

Just as I'd hoped, thank God! We pulled into Bella Luna, a quaint little joint just outside of town. The aesthetic was straight out of a movie, the sun was setting behind the restaurant which was adorned with twinkle lights around the exterior. Soft dinner music could be heard from outside the front doors setting the ambiance before you even walked in. Marcus held open the large wooden door for me and I stepped aside once I had walked in to allow him to lead the way to the attendant at the dimly lit booth ahead.

A young blonde girl, probably around 17 nervously led us to our table, nestled in a quieter and more private section of the restaurant that was strictly for reservations only.

"Your server Mario will be right with you two. Are you celebrating anything special tonight?"

"It's our first anniversary, the first of many." Marcus chimed in before I had the chance.

I felt my cheeks redden at the encounter. It was tender and sweet and all the things my girly high school self could've dreamed of.

We had been there a few times before. Marcus knew I loved it, but we had never done the reservation experience. It's been known to be just higher quality service, more seasoned servers and supposedly better food, but who's to know. I figured we would be the judge of that.

"Hi Folks, I'm Mario, I'll be your server tonight, can I get you started with some drinks from the bar? We have a great espresso martini on special tonight as well as the classic Old Fashioned. Maritza told me you guys were celebrating an anniversary tonight, congratulations, here's to many more!"

"I would like a Jameson extra sour please with an orange" I said with a meek smile. Everyone judged me but it was truly, and still is, my favorite drink when it came to alcohol. I discovered it in college, and I've stayed loyal to it since. No sense in fixing something that isn't broken, right?

" Jack and coke for me. Double shot bud, thanks."

Classic Marcus, he's always getting a double shot. He claims it saves money because he gets drunk faster, the math doesn't add up though, it's really roughly the same amount as just getting more drinks. But whatever, suit yourself Marcus, if that's what makes you happy.

"Great! I'll have those right out for you two and I'll leave you with some menus. Here's some water to hold you over in the meantime. Again, my name's Mario if you need anything."

He filled our glasses and turned on his heels with the pitcher in hand and headed back towards the bar, leaving us with just the menus and each other. A tea candle flickered in the center of the table; it rested on a little lily pad floating on water. I found myself losing focus mesmerized by its light more than once. Marcus cleared his throat and tilted his menu down to glance at me. I presumed he wanted to know if I was ever going to decide what I wanted to eat.

Mario returned and we ordered an appetizer of Focaccia. So good. I ordered a Spaghetti Alla Carbonara and Marcus ordered a Fiorentina Steak, another round of drinks as well.

The night carried on, Marcus and I spent dinner reminiscing about the past year spent together. We talked about how we met at the Stomp, our friends, old and new, moving in together, projects around the house we wanted to do, vacations we needed to plan. The conversation flowed for well over an hour, and well beyond the point that our plates had been empty. But it's our anniversary, we deserve to sit back and enjoy some time together, and the ambiance here, I can't emphasize it enough, is so welcoming and cozy. I wish I could just bottle it up and bring it home with me.

As we made our way to the car, I noticed Marcus had a tighter grasp around my waist than normal. Maybe he was feeling frisky from the three double shots of Jack, or maybe he wanted to get lucky for our anniversary when we got home. I had planned on that anyway. Either way, I wasn't sure what this was about, but I wasn't going to complain. I liked my man a little possessive once in a while.

When we arrived at our car, a white Audi A8 with all black interior, he didn't open the door for me. *Strange*, I thought to myself, but I didn't dwell on it. It's not his job after all, and the chivalrous gesture wasn't necessarily expected, but I was caught off guard. I got in before he did and began to scroll my phone to see if there was anything I'd missed during our time out. There wasn't.

"Adding Mario's number to your contacts under Kate or something over there? I saw the way he looked at you. I'm sure he slipped his number under your plate. Little faggot. I bet you loved that attention, you always do, that's why your nose is always stuck so far up your social media feeds. You live for that shit."

Woah... that alcohol really did kick in quick. Marcus has never spoken to me like that. Geez, what on Earth had gotten into him.

"Babe, what? I was just checking to see if I had any messages. That's all."

"Save it Arabella. I don't even want to hear it right now, look at you, look at what you're wearing. You dressed in the skimpiest outfit possible like you were just destined to embarrass me on our anniversary. This is why I don't take you to nice places. You just *have* to ruin it and let every guy in town eye fuck the shit out of you and make me look like a fucking cuck. That's really nice of you. I'm throwing that dress in the trash as soon as we get home. You look like a slut, and I won't be seen around with a slut. We're going home."

I felt the pressure building as the tears welled up in my eyes threatening to breach the lid and escape, but I couldn't grant him that victory. My face and neck burned, and I knew I was all different sorts of red, my hands resembled a lone leaf in the end of fall, shaking and timid. I was a hot mess, and I knew it. There was no denying it, if you looked at me you would just know I was seconds away from a monumental breakdown, but I refused to let that happen in front of him, especially not tonight. Tonight was supposed to be magical. Tonight *was* magical. Until it wasn't.

My one-year subscription of perfection seemingly expired right there before me. I wanted to rub my eyes and wish it all away, but deep inside me, I knew that wasn't going to happen. The true colors had finally come out, the man I thought I knew, and the man who sat beside me, were evidently two very different people, and all it took was 3 double shots of Jack and Coke to exacerbate that reality.

DEFEATING THE MOOSE

Who was this person, and what did I get myself into?

Chapter 5
Endless Cycles

"Where is that motherfucker?"

It didn't take a genius to know who Marcus was referring to. After all, D had just openly assaulted him plain as day, over some supposed threats Marcus had sent him. *Brilliant.*

"I said where is he?"

"I don't know. He got in his car and left. That's not my fucking problem. What did you do?"

"That doesn't fucking matter, Arabella. That's none of your damn business. Where's the bag?"

"You stuffed it in the radio console right before…"

He lifted a hand signaling me to stop talking before grabbing the little plastic baggy and inspecting it closely. He looked at it like he'd just struck gold. There were usually only two or three wax baggies rolled up in the plastic bag, this one had probably five or six.

"Guess that limp dick, pussy learned not to skimp on me this time. All i did was threaten to rape his dead mother's corpse. I didn't think it was that bad!"

"Jesus, Marcus. You're such a scumbag, you know that? Sometimes I wish I'd never left The Stomp with you. I should've just gone home."

"Well, you didn't, now did you, Doll? So, be thankful. We've made it 5 years, what's 5 more? Let's not go upsetting Daddy Marcus, you see what happens when people get on my bad side sweetheart."

"What? A broken nose and you being knocked unconscious? Sounds promising, dude."

I couldn't even deal with his arrogance. He literally just got his shit rocked and he still thinks he's hot shit. That had to be the furthest thing from the truth. I gazed out the windows of Marcus's beat up S-10. It's a miracle this thing even runs and drives I thought to myself. It was unregistered, uninsured and a ticking time bomb for every traffic ticket the cops could ever write. The AC was busted, the radio, sold for an eighth of weed, heat, never had it. This thing was a literal shit box on wheels, the only mission it purposefully served was getting to and from meetups with D and Stuart. Well, now, possibly no one. As if. There would always be *someone* looking to flip.

The truck, as if it could read my mind, sputtered and moaned as we pulled into our drive. We lived at the end of a long dirt driveway, concaves from rain washout were plastered along the entire length. Our trailer might as well have been considered no-man's-land. No one in their right mind came down our driveway, no one wanted to associate with us, mostly Marcus, but we were a package deal so that meant me too. It was a horrendous yellow color, constructed in the early 80's and was probably better off condemned. Three broken steps made of rotten wood led up to the front porch, which had at least a half dozen holes in it. You had to be careful where you stepped, or you'd risk falling right through.

One time, a few summers ago, Marcus had walked out here in the middle of a rainstorm, the wood was already soggy, but he was in a fit of rage on the phone with Zeke, his last dealer. One swift stomp down and his foot went straight through the wood up to his thigh, ripping his faded blue Levis in the process. Man, that was a night, equally as comical for me as it was infuriating for him, but I'd never let that be known.

"Home sweet home baybaaaay!" Marcus yelled in a sing-song tune prancing off to the bedroom waving the baggy around like Charlie after he'd just won Willy Wonka's fucking Golden Ticket.

"Yeah, home sweet motherfucking home alright" I thought to myself.

I kicked my shoes off at the door and headed straight to the kitchen, I swear I could have been better off with an IV drip of coffee, but that wasn't an option, so another two cups had to be made.

The process repeated itself, as it had every single day. Rinse the cup, fill the Keurig, wait for the hiss, swap the cups, add the sugar and the creamer, and stir. A never-ending cycle. My life seemed full of those these days. That and the constant sound of Marcus in the background prepping his rig. *Sigh*

"What a life"

As sure as shit is brown, I walk in the room to Marcus yet again, needle in hand, pink charger tied around his bicep, fist clenched and ready to go. I wish this ugly prick would just cut the shit already. Either quit the drugs or quit breathing. The second would probably benefit me more at this point, at least I'd finally get some peace and quiet. Without the drugs he wouldn't even know his ass from his elbow, his brain is fucking mush. The mere sight of him, and the stench emitting from him makes me feel physically ill more and more each goddamn day, I swear to God I don't even know how much more of it I can take. If he were dead maybe I could go back to my old life, have my old friends back and pretend none of this shit ever happened. Who the fuck am I kidding, I am just as stuck in this life as he is. Fucking pointless.

"This shit is fucking TOP tier Doll. Top fucking tier. Are you sure you don't want a cotton shot, I'll take it easy on you, I swear, it won't be like last time. I'll go easy, it's only fair."

"No, Marcus" I rolled my eyes so far I could nearly see the wall behind me.

"I don't want your shitty fucking drugs, I don't know why you even bother asking me, but its probably because your brain is so goddamn fried you forget everything that comes out of my mouth, that's if you even listen in the first place."

"Look bitch, I was being fucking nice, don't go acting fucking high and mighty. I promise, you ain't shit today, you weren't shit yesterday and you sure as hell won't be shit tomorrow either. Shut the fuck up and go find a cock to slobber on, maybe bring home a few fucking bucks for it so I can go find more of this. Then maybe we can be on better terms."

"Get fucked, Marcus. Get. Fucked. You're a lowlife, piece of shit, junkie and I don't know what gets your rocks off more, the fucking dope or being a douchebag to me. But my guess would be, without either, you'd fucking crumble like the little bitch that you are. So, I'll repeat it one more time for you. Get. Fucked."

Another repetitive cycle. Lick the spoon and needle clean, wrap them in the cloth, shove them behind the bed, toss the lighter to the side somewhere to complain about later, continue to be a raging asshole.

My mistake, I let my guard down a moment too long, before I could react, my already snarled hair was wrapped around Marcus' fat fingers. Off the bed I went in one swift motion and right into the wall, this time the drywall actually cracked and fell onto my shoulders as the left side of my head entered the negative space.

Without removing his right hand from my hair Marcus grabbed around my throat with his left and lifted just enough to take my weight off the ground, I could instantly feel the circulation being cut off as the pressure in my face and head built. Trying to fight back was absolutely useless. Every move I made he squeezed tighter, and now his knee was ramming into my pelvis so hard I was sure another bruise had already begun to form.

"Don't you ever disrespect me like that again cunt, you hear me? I don't know how many fucking chances I have to fucking give you, but I swear on everything holy you'll regret ever being born if you don't figure your shit out real quick. I'm not playing this fucking game with you anymore Arabella."

Marcus loosened his grip just the slightest to tease me as I gasped for air. A split second later he spit directly in my face and nailed a punch right across my left cheekbone. The world around me began to spin as he dropped me to the ground, the faded sound of him scoffing, "Bitch" was the last thing I heard before everything went black. Another endless cycle.

Chapter 6
Marcus the Accordion

Light beams invaded my eyes as they flickered open. I found myself still in the same place on the floor Marcus had left me. Dust from the drywall littered the floor around me and covered my shirt, hair, face, effectively everywhere. When I sat up, you could nearly make out a print of where I had just laid merely lifeless moments ago.

"Why the fuck ... oh right. I wouldn't take a hit with him. Fucking idiot should know better."

I wiped the dust particles out of my face and forced myself upright onto my feet. I was a bit unsteady, naturally after being choked and knocked unconscious by a behemoth of a man, so I stabilized myself against the wall until the world stopped spinning and my ears quit ringing.

"Good morning, Sunshine. Ready to quit running your fucking mouth, or are you trying to play the main role of Sleeping Beauty again?"

Wonderful, he noticed me. I mean, how wouldn't he. I look like a baby deer trying to stand up here, not exactly inconspicuous.

"No, Marcus. I'm just fucking fine. Thank you for the extra concern, but I am all set. I'm going to make a coffee do you want one?"

"Is water wet, doll? Carry on with it."

As requested, I returned with two piping hot coffees. I don't know why I even bothered asking if he'd wanted one, I guess it was just a nicety, but I already knew the answer. I had half a thought to put a teaspoon or two of bleach powder or weed killer in it, but I refrained. For now. He'd get his fix in due time. He'd be at my mercy soon enough, paying for all the shit he'd put me through. I just needed to work out a few kinks and grow some balls. Otherwise, I'd be stuck in this eternal hell space forever. That, however, was not an option.

I had sunk into the bed and allowed myself to get carried away with thoughts of all the revenge I would seek on Marcus, but he was none the wiser. I appeared just to be enjoying sipping on my cup of coffee, which, don't get me wrong, I was, but it was the inner thoughts appeasing me most.

Would I do it in his sleep? Would I do it fast, or make him suffer slowly? What would I do with his body? Could I even do this, or is this just a fantasy that I'll revel in 'til the end of time?

The latter seemed the most likely scenario, unfortunately. I was far too meek and frail to even stand up for myself never mind overpower this man and successfully rid of him without any hinges in the plan. Who was I kidding? I'd never be able to do that. *Fuck*. And just as the thoughts left my mind, the last drop of coffee left my cup. *Fuck again.*

What time even was it? Did that even matter though?

Time was nothing more than a figment of my imagination at this point. I had nowhere to go, nowhere to be, no one to see, or to visit me. Everything I did ran on Marcus' time, which was a 25/8/365 ordeal. Yes, 25/8. With Marcus, there was no 24/7, urgency was of the utmost importance to him, and he had not a single lick of patience in his body to wait for anyone.

Tending to Marcus was an around the clock, full time gig. I mean, in the meantime, where I was actually conscious and not knocked out cold by the prick.

Marcus finished his coffee, and like clockwork, reached behind the bed for the scruffy blue facecloth. This *had* to be getting worse. There was no way he could keep on like this, just dosing up round the clock with no other care in the world other than laying into me. He'd already finished off one bag since we'd gotten back this morning and was now starting to unroll a second. That only left him 4 more of the filled wax baggies.

He pulled out his spoon and licked it clean once more for good measure and began to empty a part of the contents of the second baggie onto the spoon. Not that it really made a difference, we all knew he was just going to lick it again when he was done.

He was interrupted from his ritual by the rare sound of his phone buzzing. After his falling out with D this morning, we didn't expect to be hearing from anyone today, *especially* not D of all people.

"Welcome to LaLaLand Bitch" Marcus read aloud, looking at his phone like it was some kind of foreign object he'd never laid eyes on before.

"What's that supposed to mean?"

"I don't know, Doll. That's all the text said, probably wasn't even for me. Whatever. He's a pussy anyways. I'm not responding, fuck him."

"Okay then, weird."

DEFEATING THE MOOSE

Like nothing ever happened, Marcus went right back to business. He twisted the top off the water bottle beside him, withdrew a squirt of water with the needle, and dropped a few drops onto the spoon along with the white powder he added before the text came in. As he twisted the top back on the bottle with one hand, he pulled my pink charger out of the wall with the other, unplugging my phone and tossing it back to me in the process.

"Here, go look at some dick pics if you're not going to join me."

Eye roll.

I swiped open my phone and tapped on the Monopoly-Go app, it was my guilty pleasure when Marcus actually let me use my phone without a fuss.

Marcus dropped a used wad of cotton onto the spoon before flicking the lighter and holding it just below the surface and waving it back and forth. He pushed the contents of the spoon around a bit with the needle tip before the familiar crackle indicating it was ready and about to boil. He placed the needle between his front teeth; a trick he'd adapted to make it easier to do everything at once and get the job done quicker. Then, he grabbed the barrel with the hand that had already been holding the lighter and lowered his head down until the needle tip was submerged in the cotton soaked in the now murky brown liquid on the spoon. He pulled back until there was no liquid left floating and it was all loaded in the rig. He placed the spoon down on the floor between his feet, licked the tip of the needle, and then flicked the barrel and depressed a single drop of the precious substance to make sure there were no air bubbles.

Now that the needle wasn't in his mouth, he pulled one end of my charger tight between his jaws, and held the other end with the same hand, creating an unbelievably tight noose around his arm, you could already see the veins starting to bulge. It's not like you really had to look for them though, there was a perfect road map tracked across his inner elbow already in deep blues and purples from the overuse. His breathing got heavier as he made a fist and shakily pushed the needle into his vein. He pulled back on the plunger until there was blood in the syringe, ensuring proper placement and he was ready for takeoff. He pushed the entirety of the contents deep into his vein, slowly but steadily.

With each moment, you could almost see more and more life leaving his eyes until the syringe was as empty as his expression. I knew what this meant. Not even seconds later and Marcus was slumped forward, 'sucking his own dick' as he called it when he saw other tweakers nodded out. It was a fair statement though, the way he folded in on himself like an accordion, it did look like he was, in fact, sucking his own dick.

Better him than me, I guess.

I'm not sure if I was in denial, or just so used to it at this point, but I knew, or thought I knew at least, that he'd stir awake eventually, once the effects started to wear off. I gave him a nudge for good measure but honestly, I didn't have the fucking motivation, nor the encouragement to do any more than that.

Why would he even deserve that much? Not like he'd do the same for me. He's made that vividly clear. I'm just a toss aside to him, a punching bag and the sounding board for all of his useless banter. I was tired of being his puppet.

So yeah, the courtesy nudge, that was the most he was going to get out of me today, or ever again. In fact, I pray he doesn't even wake up.

"Man, I'm begging you, just keep his crusty ass this time, dude. Do me a fucking solid for ONCE" I whispered to myself, pleading to whatever god or external force would

listen to me, chances are, none, but what's the use in not trying?

Manifest that shit, right? That's what the girls are saying, or doing these days? "Claiming" and "manifesting" everything into the universe. Well, I *don't* claim him, and I want to manifest him *out* of the universe.

He stayed folded in half another five minutes before I decided to help myself to the kitchen to find a snack, coffee couldn't hold me off forever. I was sure he'd be awake by the time I came back; he *always* was.

Chapter 7
Beer, Cashews, and Blood

I managed to find a Bud Light tucked in the back corner of the fridge. How long had that been there? I am certain it wasn't there the hundred other times I've come here this week.

Whatever. Bottoms up, I suppose.

A half empty canister of Planters honey roasted whole cashews sat in the cabinet calling my name also. I cracked open the beer and canister of nuts leaving the lid on the counter and aimlessly sauntered towards the kitchen window. The first sip of the beer told me without any regard that the beer was old, but I couldn't let it go to waste now. I still don't understand how I never noticed it in the back of the fridge either, but that's neither here nor there at this point. A drink was a drink, and it was something more than coffee so it would have to do.

I stared off at the sky. Contrails and big fluffy clouds spread across the expanse of the horizon, or as far as my eyes could see at least. It was easy to get lost in the sight, a welcome distraction to my current living hell. I almost forgot where I was, dazing off in the distance, sipping the stale beer and shoving fistfuls of cashews into my mouth unconsciously. By the looks of it, I was a malnourished dog experiencing a T-bone steak for the first time. I mean hell, I'd been surviving off adrenaline and coffee for the better part of two days now.

Not a moment too soon in my moment of peace and glory, I snapped back to reality, acknowledging the gravity of the silence in the trailer. A deafening, uncomfortable silence. A pit formed in my stomach as I came to the realization that I still hadn't heard Marcus stir back to life. He wasn't cursing my name into the wind, no clanking of metal or rustling as he stuffed the equipment behind the bed. It had been far too long now for this much silence. That could only mean one thing. This silence was here to stay.

A bead of sweat dripped down the back of my neck as I flipped the half empty beer upside down in the sink. I wouldn't be finishing that. I tried to calm my mind, convince myself he had simply fallen asleep, just like this morning. I shook the last of the cashews into my mouth before chucking the empty container into the bin beside the sink. It dawned on me that I was prolonging the inevitable, avoiding the truth I already knew. I was procrastinating returning to the room. But why?

Did a part of me actually care right now? Was this some polar vortex or alternate universe that I'd stepped into when I left the room the last time?

I already knew what I'd find when I walked back into that room, so why should I even bother doing it? What purpose did that even serve me? But like a nagging fly that evades every swat, some unseen force leading me towards the hallway, to the bedroom.

The shaking in my hands amplified with each step I took towards the back room. By the time I made it there it felt like my entire body might just vibrate into a different dimension. My knuckles were white from the fists I didn't even realize had become balled up. I walked in the door and what the fuck do you know? Marcus was still there, slumped in the same damn position. Just like I knew he would be.

"Useless, selfish, good-for-nothing dick" the voice in my head moaned.

In that moment, something snapped in me.

A guttural scream escaped my throat, surprising even myself. I don't know if it was shock, fear, anger, resentment, or all of the above, but there was some definite gusto hidden behind those octaves I reached. I didn't stop screaming until my throat was raw and my voice was cracking. I must have blacked out somewhere along the line because the next thing I knew, I was on top of Marcus who was now laying on his back.

Every empty promise, every threat, every hit, every last venomous word he ever spoke, you name it, was being plowed into his head from every angle by my now bloody and tattered fists. I couldn't stop myself. Each punch landed harder and harder, each moment I became more and more tired, more weak, more disassociated. But I *still* couldn't stop.

"You fucking asshole! You goddamn useless bastard. Just look what you've gone and done now! You fucking did it this time Marcus, you fucking won. You won! It's fucking over now, fuck you. You selfish! Fucking! Prick!"

The words spewed out of me as tears drenched my face and blood covered every surface around me. His nose had been lessened to a flattened pile of cartilage, flesh and blood smeared mucus snots. He looked more like a pug than a junkie douchebag at this point. But I *still* couldn't stop.

I told you, something in me snapped. I ripped the needle from his arm, a shock it even remained there after the storm of fury I just released, but it did. One blow after another I jabbed it into his neck, the first shot to his Adam's apple and the tip of the needle lodged in and never released when I pulled back the barrel. Now I was just leaving holes, his neck no more than a human version of Swiss cheese. Thick blood oozed from every single gaping wound, pooling around him. I just kept on slamming the barrel of the needle into his lifeless body until it ultimately snapped under the pressure. I threw it to the ground beside me and huffed with utter exasperation.

" God I fucking hate you Marcus, why did you do this to us? I fucking loved you, you selfish prick. What the fuck! What the fuck do I do now you useless fuck? Why'd you go and do this shit to me! I fucking hate you!"

"Quit running that pretty little mouth of yours Doll, you know those dick suckers could be put to much better use than bitching..." I could hear his words taunting me, echoing within the walls of my imagination. I covered my ears and squeezed tight, begging for it to stop. Even beaten to a pulp he was still tormenting me,

"Don't you ever disrespect me like that again cunt, you hear me? .... I'm not playing this fucking game with you anymore Arabella."

"Make it *stop!* Just fucking stop I can't handle this!"

My head throbbed as I held my ears tighter and squeezed my eyes closed willing this all to just be a dream. I wished I'd just wake up, another black eye from Marcus knocking me out and he'd still be there, talking his shit.

My screams became quieter and more desperate, being replaced only by more sobs in their place. Finally, I was worn out. My body collapsed onto his chest, my entire weight heaving sighs and desperate sobs into his blood-soaked shirt. I had no fight left in me.

It was over. All of it was over. My fight, my hell, Marcus, the drugs, all of it. It was over.

A sigh of relief washed over me as I pulled myself off of Marcus and took a step back. The room had become a mausoleum of macabre and mayhem. Blood splattered the walls, the sheets ripped from the sides of the bed, Marcus' unfinished coffee slung across the floorboards. Shattered pieces of the needle everywhere. The dope spoon, now crusty, still laid on the floor alongside the bed with the lighter.

Where do I go from here? What's next? I didn't think that far.

"Shit! Shit shit shit shit shit!"

This was a disaster in so many more ways than one. I paced back and forth three or four times running my fingers through my sweat laden hair, then kicked him hard one time straight in the face. The sickening crunch and slop noises that collided with my foot was gag inducing and I nearly lost the beer and cashews all over the floor in front of me.

"Don't bother asking what the fuck that one was for. I'll let you think about it."

I chuckled to myself as I paced the floor a few more times before walking out of the room, out of this hell, out of this nightmare. A sinister thought crossed my mind causing me to pause in my tracks. I stopped and turned around, walking back to the room. There was one more thing I needed. Marcus' phone.

"Hey sexy, its Arabella. You still wanna treat me better than Marcus ever did? He's gone now, you won't have to worry about him anymore. I made sure of that. *Winky face emoji*"

Text sent. *Now* I could walk out of that nightmare.

Chapter 8
"Birthdays Were the Worst Days"

"What in the holy fuck are you wearing, Arabella? Are you a fucking prostitute or are you my girlfriend? Jesus Christ."

"Marcus, it's my birthday and I'm going out with Lynn and Marie, you know that. I've had this night planned for months and you planned nothing, so I'll be back later. I'm not wasting my night here doing nothing, listening to you piss and moan about everything under the sun on MY birthday."

"Well that sure didn't answer the fucking question, now did it, bitch? When will you be home? You better wash the cum out of your fuck hole before you get here. I don't want to smell all those random motherfuckers that just dumped their load in you when you get back. And Arabella, tell Lynn and Marie I hate those stupid cunts why don't you?"

"I don't understand your issue with them, Marcus. Would you just lay off? They've done nothing to you. You only hate them because they were there first."

"Whatever you say Arabella, I'm not going to fucking go tit for tat with you. Toss me my bowl and get out of my face. I'll see you later."

***

"Birthday, it's your birthday. When I die bury me inside a Gucci store"

The girls were already screaming at the top of their lungs as they pulled onto my street. It only got progressively louder with each house they passed in succession to mine. Marie was driving in 'Shelby', and Lynn was already half in the bag. I was determined not to let Marcus' statements put a damper on my night. After all, it was my 23rd birthday No one cares about 23, so I had to, right?

"Hop in bitch, we're *not* going shopping!"

Classic Lynn, throwing in a spin on a Mean Girls quote whenever possible.

"How's the birthday girl?"

"We haven't talked much today. What'd you do? We need all the details!"

"Did you get birthday sex? Did he get you anything?"

The girls were rapidly firing questions at me before I even had the chance to buckle my seatbelt and say hello.

"Well, hi to you too bitches, and no, no birthday sex, no gifts, going out tonight with you guys *was* my gift. He's up to his shit again, we actually just got into it over my outfit before y'all got here. But whatever, let's go have fun, I don't want to think about him. Consider me single for the night, too bad it's not for fucking ever."

"Fuck him Bells, let's go!"

And we took off as the girls waved their middle fingers out the sunroof hoping Marcus might see.

"You look fucking hot tonight, Bells" Marie said.

"Yeah! Cheers to hot Bells!" Lynn yelled as she raised her bottle of Pink Whitney in the air as if she were giving a toast.

It made me chuckle, at least someone, or two people, wanted me to have a good birthday. But two is better than none, so I took it as a win. They were right, we had barely seen each other or talked lately. Marcus *hated* them with passion, for no reason whatsoever other than simply, because he did.

We started our night getting some fries from McDonald's, we only wanted something light to be in our stomachs before we danced the night away, we knew we couldn't drink with an empty stomach though. Marie wasn't going to drink since she was the DD so she had a nugget meal as well. I did steal one though, as a birthday gift of course.

Shelby rolled into The Stomp, and we found our usual parking spot. It was about 9:15 so we already knew there'd be no tables but that was fine, we didn't intend on sitting much anyways, tonight we were going all out. Lynn passed me the bottle of Pink Whitney before we walked in, she loved pregaming to save on our bill at the end of the night.

"Cheers to you, bitch. Tonight and 23 are going to treat you right. Bottoms up, baby!"

Two swigs and I was ready to go. I could feel my face flush immediately as the liquor hit the back of my throat and the burn traveled all the way down with it.

"Uck, I don't know how you drink that shit Lynn, my god."

I gagged once and Lynn threw her head back laughing. We got out of the car, gave our ID's and debit cards to Marie to put in her wallet and we headed to the door. Just before we stepped in Marie pulled a hot pink and sparkly birthday sash out of her back pocket and draped it over my shoulders before we walked in.

"That's more like it. Let's go bitches!" she exclaimed with a Cheshire Cat smile from ear to ear.

I switched my phone to silent, there was not a chance in the world I was letting Marcus ruin this night for me more than he already had. I handed that to Marie too. "What a good mother hen." I thought to myself with a grin.

It felt like no time had passed, we were all having so much fun but before we knew it the bar was clearing out and the new bartender was yelling for last call.

"It's already midnight? Oh my God I have to get home. Marcus is going to kill me."

"Fuck him, Bells. Did you have a good night?"

"Yes, but –"

"No but's, that's all that matters. Deal with his dumb ass when you get home."

"That's what you don't understand, Marie." I started to explain as the fear and guilt started pooling in my gut.

"What's that supposed to mean?"

"Nothing let's just go. I gotta get home. I'm sorry guys."

My anxiety was building the whole drive back to our apartment. I thought my heart might actually beat right out of my chest and if my hands shook any more, I might not even be able to open the door. I smoothed my hair down and frantically wiped at the makeup below my eyes in the rearview mirror as we pulled up.

"Arabella, what's going on, are you okay? Here's your cards, babe. Do you want to come back to the apartment with us?"

"No I'm alright. Thank you for the ride and thank you both for tonight. Seriously, it means a lot."

I forced a smile and stepped out of the car. I waved as they pulled away, but part of me silently begged they'd stop part way down the road and watch to make sure I made it in. They didn't.

I braced myself for whatever was to come on the other side of the door, the lump in my throat thickening and my mouth was now dryer than the Sahara Desert. I shook my hands trying to clear the anxiety, wishing I could just shake it away and things would be perfectly fine when I walked in. I imagined he'd be in the room, candles lit, a gift on my side of the bed and a kiss waiting for me.

"Fat chance Arabella" I nearly laughed at that fantasy as I reached for the knob.

It's *locked*. He locked me out! What the fuck!

I walked around the back to check that door but as expected it was also locked.

What the fuck.

The lights were still on, so I knew he was awake. He just wanted to make a point. He *always* wanted to make a point, and *always* had to have the last laugh.

"Marcus come on; unlock the door this isn't funny." I shouted as I banged on the windowpanes of the front door.

I didn't even hear movement coming from the other side, annoying. I banged and banged and banged for what felt like hours. My phone? Why didn't I think of my phone? "Jesus, Arabella come on." I whispered to myself as I pulled up his contact.

Voicemail.

Voicemail.

Voice. Mail.

He ignored my calls 5 more times before he finally answered.

"What Arabella?"

"Open the door Marcus, it's cold outside and I have to pee. Please."

"Oh, you call the shots now? That's cute. How about you come on in here and make me? Oh wait"

Laughter erupted from the other end of the phone at a sickening pitch.

"Please Marcus, I'm sorry. Please just open the door and let me in. I love you. I'm sorry" I pleaded.

He finally unlatched the deadbolt and whipped the door open. I didn't even have both feet through the threshold before he was dragging me in by my hair.

"That is the *LAST* time you see those hoes, you hear me? The *LAST*. That's final. What the fuck is this shit? It's nearly 1am."

"I know Marcus, I'm sorry, we lost track of time –"

"What having a fucking birthday train run on you for fuck's sake? My god."

He let go of my hair and I rushed towards the bathroom. I was starting to sweat fearing my bladder would let go at any moment if he hadn't let me go soon.

"Chugga chugga choo choo!" He taunted.

"Make sure you clean out that nasty little slit of yours too, and don't you dare think for one second I'm putting my prick anywhere near you tonight. You can sleep your happy ass on the couch. Happy Birthday hoe, hope it was worth it."

As soon as the bathroom door shut behind me, the floodgates opened wide, and the tears flowed like the Nile River. I turned on the shower to drown out the sound of my cries. Not that he'd care anyway. He's probably getting some sick enjoyment out of it. "Juicy" by Notorious B.I.G. blared in my head as a stark reminder, "Birthdays was the worst days." Thanks Biggie

"Why did I put up with this?" I asked myself, pounding my fists on the bathroom floor. "I can still get out of this. I *have* to."

If only I knew then.

If only.

Chapter 9
Definitely NOT a Set-up

"Sup Doll? Whatchu mean 'I made sure of it'? How'd you even get my number... if you're serious meet me down at the lake at 8 and you better be alone. If this is a set up, you'll be sorry."

"Definitely not a setup, he's gone for good. I kicked his ass to the curb, if you will. Hoping to see what you're packing and if you're man enough for the job if you catch my drift. See you at 8, I'm looking forward to it."

"Bet. 8 it is. See you then Dollface."

I looked down at my clock, already 4:45. Time was flying by, but I had enough time to do what I had to do before meeting D. This had to go perfectly according to plan, one wrong move and everything would be over. But by tonight, my plan would begin, and revenge would be mine.

"I'll tear down the whole motherfucking chain if I have anything to say about it." I cackled to myself.

Thoughts raced in my head. Marcus was dead, like really, really, dead. Not just a little dead... all the way dead. I needed my revenge; I needed it more than I needed anything other than coffee at this point. Speaking of, I could really use a fucking coffee right now. For fucks sake, what is wrong with me? I just beat the piss out of Marcus' very dead body, and I'm concerned with coffee? Get a grip bitch... come on, focus. I *needed* to take down the whole chain of command, to seek my own justified restitution. To pay off the metaphorical debt for the years of hell I suffered at the hands of these dealers and shmucks.

The shaking that consumed my whole body had finally settled, the sweat stopped pouring down my forehead and my heart was no longer beating a million times a minute. Calm and collected, yeah right, but let's fake it. I walked back into the back bedroom where Marcus, or the mush that used to be Marcus at least, lay. The smell was already beginning to settle in the room and burn my nostrils some. I made a mental note to remember to open the windows when I came back tonight. I still needed to figure out what I was even going to do with his dumb ass, but I didn't have time for that now, I had to run, I just needed a few supplies first.

DEFEATING THE MOOSE

I went though a mental inventory in my head of what I'd need from the house.

"Marcus' phone."
"My phone."
"Dope."
"Lighter"
"Needles"
"Spoon"

"Fuck the cotton, that shit wont matter worth of shit for this job, nor will the charger," I paused, distracted by my own thoughts.

"Coffee – can't forget coffee" I continued to myself.
"Wallet, mine *and* his"
"Keys to the fucking clunker."
"Check, check and check, well... that about sums it up I guess."

I "tripped" over Marcus making my way to the closet, and by tripped what I really mean is I stomped across his torso and then slid through the slick blood on the floor beside him.

"Oops, sorry baby, didn't see you there, please forgive me, I'll make that up to you later I swear. You look so handsome today, I sure didn't mean it baby, you gotta believe me."

I winked at him for good measure and continued towards the closet. The devil on my shoulder was growing bigger and more menacing with each passing moment.

I was still covered in his blood so I would most definitely need a second shower, and new clothes before heading to the store. I stripped down out of the dirty clothes and tossed them into the pool of blood hoping it would soak up at least some of the mess, another problem for later I didn't have time for right now. Every article of clothing on me, right into the puddle with a sick, sloshing, splash. I grabbed a fresh outfit, one of very few I did have, and wasted precisely no time getting in the shower. I was in a serious time crunch if this was going to work.

It was 5:30 by the time I was out of the shower, brushed my hair and got dressed. I chose a pair of tight black leggings that cupped my ass generously and a crop hoodie from college. I needed something with sleeves tonight but also something that drew enough attention to my body to be distracting." Calm and collected, right Arabella?"

I looked around the house one last time and walked out the door by 5:45, where had the time gone so quickly? Luckily for me, there was a Tractor Supply about 15 minutes from the trailer, they would have the rest of the supplies I needed before tonight's festivities got under way.

Upon entering the store, I kept my head down and made my way straight to the back where the equestrian care supplies were kept. It didn't take me long to find the 22-gauge needles. They were in a 5 pack, this couldn't have been more perfect already, and they were much cheaper than I had expected them to be, so that's even better! Next up was a horse tranquilizer, Acepromazine. 50ml was $34. A little pricey but still better than nothing, it would be playing a pivotal role in the remainder of my night after all. It did dawn on me that cashing out with just needles and horse tranquilizers might seem a little suspicious, I highly doubt I looked like I had any business purchasing those supplies whatsoever. Fingers crossed and hoping for the best at least.

"Is there anything I can help you find, miss?"

A young associate had come up behind me startling me for a moment rendering me speechless.

"Oh, no thank you, my sister owns a couple horses and one of them isn't doing so well so she asked me to pick up some supplies and bring them by since she can't leave the farm. Could you just let me know if you guys sell any chocolate pretzels? I know that probably sounds crazy considering the rest of my cart's contents, but I missed out on lunch today."

"Yeah, no problem, they're right by the register to the right, I hope everything goes over well with your sister. If you need me, I'll just be up front, the name's Jason."

Well, *that was close...* He looked innocent and naïve enough, he probably bought every second of that luckily. I found the chocolate pretzels and saw that Jason's register was open, so I hurried to that one to save face before having to awkwardly explain myself to anyone else.

""Will that be cash or card? I didn't get your name I apologize."

"It's Leah, and it'll be cash, thank you."

"Pleasure meeting you Leah, that'll be $37.20 today. And again, good luck with your sister, that's never easy to deal with."

I handed Jason $40 and told him to save the change for the next customer. I put my head back towards the floor and made a beeline to the door, I didn't want to spend any more time in that store than I needed to, besides, it was getting late, I *had* to get moving.

I ripped open the bag of chocolate pretzels and placed them on the passenger's seat so I could snack on them during the 35-minute trek ahead of me. The lake was about 20 minutes the opposite direction of town, by the time I arrived there, it would be after 7 and I still had to get gas as well, I couldn't risk running out.

By 7:20 I was pulling up into the lake, I chose a secluded area in the back of the lot, plenty of privacy, and the way the lot was set, up no curious onlookers could see inside the cars from any direction. We would look like nothing more than a couple teenagers smoking some weed or getting their rocks off.

"Little did they know" I laughed.

I set everything out onto the center console to prepare it. First, I drew 10ml of the sedative into the syringe, to give it that one last punch needed, and made sure to leave plenty of room for the dope. I threw the bottle into the glove box; I didn't want to be immediately seen with that if anything happened. Not that any of this was any better. I looked at the clock, 7:25. I had to slow down, there was too much time left. I decided to open Tiktok on my phone and scroll my "for you page" and snack on the chocolate pretzels, I'd come back to this sadistic science experiment soon enough.

At 7:43 I figured it would be a good time to get the ball rolling again. If I waited too long, I risked him pulling in early, and this definitely wasn't going to be the hangout he was anticipating. On the other hand, if I started too soon, the liquids in the spoon would thicken too much and I would risk clogging the syringe. Luckily the horse syringe being 22-gauge should alleviate *some* of that, at least I hoped so. This next part, I'd seen Marcus do eighty-eight thousand times so it would be like playing follow the leader, but I would be the only winner.

I emptied the entire contents of the baggie onto the spoon. D was my first, so I had to make it extra special for him of course. I squirted a few drops of the tranquilizer onto the spoon to mix with the dope to liquify it and lit the fire underneath the spoon. Like I said, the cotton wouldn't matter tonight, so I just went straight to drawing the liquid into the syringe, not wasting a single drop of this sacred concoction. I drew back a little extra air as well, we all know air bubbles are no bueno, which for me meant very bueno tonight.

Once I was content, I stored all but the needle in my center console. I pulled up my right sleeve and positioned the syringe along my forearm and secured it in place with a hair elastic. I had to be insanely careful so I wouldn't poke myself. I pulled my sleeve down just as I saw headlights entering my rearview mirror.

"It's showtime" I said aloud and took a deep breath. I pulled my sun visor down and started smoothing my hair out of my face trying to look as inconspicuous and natural as possible. As expected, D pulled up beside Marcus' beat to shit S-10 and gave a few precautionary glances before shutting off the engine.

I stepped out of the car and noticed his passenger window was already open, I wonder if it even rolled up. I never saw it up any other time.

"So, he's really not with you, huh? He's not hiding out in a bush somewhere thinking hes going to ambush me or something?"

"No D, he's gone." I laughed to myself, and it came out a smidge creepier than intended, hopefully he didn't notice that.

"Shit, okay then doll hop in the back seat."

Fuck, he just made this easier for me all on his own.

Chapter 10
The Meetup Pt. 2

Without wasting any time I climbed into David's backseat, I didn't have much time to waste anyhow. The car smelled of old French fries and cheap cologne. This better go over quickly.

"Sup Doll? So you got rid of him finally huh?"

"Uh yeah. He's actually *dead*"

You could literally see the blood drain from his face as he began to resemble more of a ghost. A deep, throaty, chuckle erupted from him accompanied by a toothy grin that showed off his grill that definitely looked like it was done in some sketchy ass back alley.

"So, my little game of Russian Roulette worked."

"Your what?"

"Oh I gave him extra bags. Only one was clean, the rest were laced. I was sick of his shit. Looks like luck wasn't in his favor today, huh?"

"Damn, that's hot. So whatchu packin?"

"Why don't you get those pretty little lips down here and find out for yourself, sweetheart."

David unbuttoned his jeans and slid them halfway down his thighs along with his bright orange boxers. Immediately a mediocre dick peaked out from behind a whole bush of pubic hair like some kind of crooked ass jack-in-the-box with an afro. It would take some commercial grade hedge trimmers to get past that. Damn, didn't expect that for a man who tries so hard to show off.

I leaned down, keeping my right arm accessible but remaining ever so cautious not to poke myself. I took his length in my left hand and pushed the hair back to the base to the best of my ability while I tried not to show my disdain.

"You like that baby? Don't hold back, gimme all you got."

"Oh yeah big boy, I'll do just that. Don't you worry." Snickered the devil on my shoulder who was basically doing cartwheels and jumping jacks at this point.

"Oh I will, just you sit right there and enjoy and I'll do the same." I shot him a wink and leaned down taking my final gasp of air before showtime.

DEFEATING THE MOOSE

My mouth was salivating already, threatening to make me gag right there on the spot before even getting started. I squeezed my thumb in my right fist to try and counter that, it's an old wives' tale, don't judge me. I loosened my jaw and swallowed as much of his shaft as I could, I wanted to start off strong and get the ball rolling. I pulled back releasing David's mediocre dick from my mouth and let the drool spill out over him. I wiped my lip, spit the remainder of my saliva onto the tip of his dick and slicked my left hand down from top to bottom. I saw his head start to fall back in ecstasy and I knew this was my moment.

I began moaning as I sucked his cock to hide any sounds and create a distraction. I wiggled the needle loose from my sleeve and held it tightly in my right hand beside the seat out of his view in case he happened to snap back to reality and look up. Without missing a beat, I lifted my mouth from his cock once more and began stroking him as if it were a simple hand job in between sucking his dick. In one swift motion as I pulled his foreskin towards his tip with my left hand, I jabbed the needle into his taint as hard as I could and depressed the plunger as quick as possible with my right sending the entirety of the concoction straight into him.

"God I hope that fucking worked" the pesky little devil said unwaveringly.

D's eyes bulged, nearly leaving their sockets. He tried to yell and gasp for air but it was a fleeting moment before his eyes rolled back and he was silent. Just how I like it.

"Sorry, you ugly prick, but thanks for being such a wonderful contestant on today's show!"

I sure hoped that what I'd given him was enough. I had no idea, but I certainly wasn't prepared on the off chance that it wasn't. I was, however, in the perfect position to make this look entirely accidental. As far as anyone could tell, the poor ole boy came down to the lake, started beating his meat, shot up and unfortunately overdosed. Simple as that.

To air on the side of caution, I took the needle out from under his dick and placed it in his hand. The cops around here would be none the wiser, to them it's just another dealer off the streets, they had zero interest in *actually* looking into this. At least not yet, I had a safe few days to spare to finish what I'd started.

I checked out the back windshield to check for any new cars, luckily, there were none. I reached into the front and grabbed D's phone and wallet. I also found another pre-packed stash in the center console. I pocketed a handful of the wax baggies before slipping out of the backseat. I figured I wouldn't need too many, I still had some of what Marcus had, and a handful was at least 20 baggies, that would be plenty to do some damage.

My stomach grumbled, those chocolate pretzels were calling my name, and I was desperate to get the stale taste of D out of my mouth immediately. I'd definitely need to find some real food soon if I was going to keep this up, Lord knows there's nothing in the trailer and it's not like Marcus is coming home with anything for us anytime soon either. I climbed in my front seat and began blasting Cooper Allen's rendition of Colt 45 as I shifted the S-10 into gear and pulled away. The engine whined incessantly, and I laughed hysterically.

This was going to be much easier than I expected.

Chapter 11
Revenge Rendezvous Pt. 1

Sure as motherfucking shit something just *had* to happen, didn't it? I was about 50 yards from the street entrance when a cloud of dust plumed up in front of me blocking my view, and the sound of squealing tires was almost deafening surrounding me from every direction.

"What the *fuck?*" I stammered to myself, my eyes darting from side to side attempting to make sense of the situation.

When the smoke cleared, I found myself the bullseye in a weird roundup of four beat up Civics and Subarus. I still had no clue what the hell was going on, but I didn't like it one bit. It dawned on me, in a moment of fleeting clarity, that Marcus had a loaded Beretta BB gun under the front seat. He said he never needed a 'real' gun. He didn't want lethal, he just wanted to disable the other person enough to have the upper hand to win 'fair and square' because he's 'not a pussy'. And for once, I actually agreed with him. I didn't want to kill them all instantly. I wanted my revenge; I just didn't foresee this being part of the plan.

I reached down, trying to remain as inconspicuous as possible, keeping my eyes locked scanning back and forth all around me. My hand found the cold, hard, handle and my fingers curled around it. It was heavier than I expected it to be, considering how small it was, but it fit in my hand like it was crafted just for me. I up righted myself and took a deep, steadying breath trying to shake as little as possible. It had only been moments since they pulled up on me, but it felt like it had been a solid ten minutes.

"No fucking way…" I thought to myself out loud, "this can not be happening right now."

Almost in unison, stepping out of each car, was Stuart, Zeke, a guy I vaguely recognized as another big wig dealer, Diego, and another dude I'd never seen before. This could not be good news.

Before I could spare another second wondering what this little rendezvous was about, Stuart shouted out loud enough to rattle through me even with the windows of the S-10 up.

"Listen up, Marcus, you little cuck bitch, get the fuck out of that shit can and we can talk this over like real men. Did you think any of us really believed your little slut girlfriend was coming here to meet up with D? Where the fuck even is David? I see his car right there, so where the fuck is he?"

With my left hand gripping the Beretta and my right hand on the window button, I prepared myself for what was going to happen next, whatever that may be, but I sure the fuck wasn't going down without a fight I knew that much.

"I'm gonna give your faggot ass one more chance to get the fuck out of that truck, or we're going to rip you out right now and skin your ass right here on the ground."

"Well, they sound pretty serious," I contemplated, "but unfortunately, they're all out of their vehicles and currently empty handed. So, the math to me, looked a lot like I already had the advantage."

I rolled the window down halfway and threw the truck into drive. In a split second, I squeezed my eyes as I gunned it towards the stranger of the group. He held the least importance, so cutting him out had no catharsis for me. He was just collateral.

I felt the collision almost immediately, and I brought the car to a halt as the brakes screamed. I looked in the rearview just as his limp body finished its free flight through the air and skidded across the gravel like a flat rock on a lake.

Stuart and Zeke rushed to the lifeless man, and I could see Diego turning to come my way. Frantic, inaudible screams filled the air but it was quickly cut with three quick pops from the BB gun in my hand. I didn't even remember putting my hand out the window, never mind pulling the trigger, but apparently, my subconscious actions deemed me a pretty sharpshooter. Diego instantly doubled over, holding his face as blood began spraying the entire surface around him. He looked up and it was evident he was in rough shape. Perfect.

"Motherfucker's got a gun? When the fuck did Marcus get a gun?" Stuart shouted.

One down, for now, two to go.

Stuart and Zeke looked like little chickens running around with their heads cut off. They didn't know if they should stay with the man or rush to Diego's side next. For good measure, I actually aimed this time with the brief moment I had and fired one more shot directly at Diego. I wasn't sure where it hit him initially, but when he fell to the ground, a new trail of blood began oozing out of his left ear. Before he even hit the ground Stuart and Zeke were on their feet and stumbling towards me.

"What the fuck, man? What is wrong with you? Chill the fuck out!" Zeke barely managed to get out with a shrill screech hidden behind his words.

"David! Where the fuck are you, brother? Get the fuck out here!"

Stuart must've had a second thought because as Zeke remained on his path, Stuart veered left and made a beeline to David's car. *Oh, this is gonna be good,* I thought to myself with a laugh. I could handle this; I could really do this.

Ego got the best of me, and I hopped out of the car. The look on Zeke's face was absolutely priceless.

"Surprise, douchebag. It was really me. I let Marcus die, I killed David's ugly ass, and I'm gonna kill you sick fucks too. And then... and then, Zeke, you know what I'm gonna do next? I'm gonna sit here and enjoy my fucking chocolate pretzels and enjoy the rest of my fucking night too. *That* is what I'm *gonna* do. Surprise!"

I raised the Beretta in his direction and, before he could beg for his poor pitiful fucking life, I drilled five shots straight into his face. He dropped backwards immediately and fell unconscious.

"Well, that was anticlimactic." I said out loud. I wonder if they all think this is a real gun. I mean from a distance, it looks no different than one. Works out in my favor that's for certain. Big dogs become real fucking puppies when faced with a gun and they're empty handed.

I remembered Marcus saying he liked the Beretta; it held seventeen BB's and that was his favorite number. I already laid out nine, so I had eight left. I had to make them worth it.

Stuart looked over his shoulder briefly just as he made it to David's car, but I think shock set in because he stayed where he was at. The sound of Diego moaning in pain in the background was music to my ears.

I took about ten steps, and I was now towering over Zeke's blood-smeared face. I squatted down with a wicked smile, placed the barrel into his open mouth and pulled the trigger twice more. I stood up and with every ounce of might I had, I stomped down onto Zeke's straining throat. *Six bullets left.*

"Now that's more like it."

Just as my foot left Zeke's neck a guttural scream escaped from beside David's car. This was fucking beautiful, but I wasn't done yet.

Chapter 12
Revenge Rendezvous Pt. 2

"Are you fucking kidding me?"

"David"

"NO"

Stuart's pleas fell on empty ears and continued relentlessly.

"He's dead, dumbass. That may come as a surprise to you, but so is Marcus, Zeke, your little friend over there and well, by the looks of things, Diego isn't looking, or sounding too fucking hot himself either. Looks like you're a lone wolf out here now, pal."

"Arabella, come on. What the fuck? Why are you doing _"

"Save it, moron. I let Marcus die, then beat the piss out of his dead body. I sent your little friend for a goddamn skydiving adventure. I just face fucked Zeke with a handful of these bullets. And Diego, well, it wasn't supposed to be that quick and lousy, but it was. As for you, I'm not sure what I'll do with you yet. I'm just getting started. None of this was part of tonight's plan. You guys just *had* to come down here and crash my little party with your brother. What a shame, he took a needle full of dope and horse tranqs right to the dick. Unfortunate."

Stuart held his hands out like a preacher mid-sermon and began sauntering towards me.

"Take one more fucking step and I'll blow your foot clean off."

I knew it wasn't true, a BB gun was never going to do that. It was an utter shock it accumulated the amount of damage and bloodshed that it had already. I wasn't placing bets I knew I couldn't win.

Unfortunately for Stuart, he wanted to test the theory.

"Six bullets" I repeated in my head. I lifted the Beretta with my left hand. Comically, Stuart tried to turn and run just as I pulled the trigger. It landed directly behind his right kneecap. He stumbled for a few steps, but being a man of his stature, I knew it wouldn't disable him long; if at all. He was the biggest of the bunch both in height and weight.

"Son of a bitch, Arabella. Goddamn, fucking stop!"

"And why should I do that, Stuart? Do tell me. Make my day."

"What the fuck did I ever do to you? What did ANY of us do to you?"

"Well, you see, here's the thing. You and your fucking circus puppets decided putting goddamn dope and Lord knows what else into innocent hands. THEN, David decided he was going to play some fucked up game of Russian Roulette with Marcus. Fun fact: he fucking lost. Which in retrospect is neither here nor there. It benefitted me in the long run, but this all could've been fucking avoided. You knew exactly what every single one of you were doing putting that shit out on the streets, ruining lives, ripping families apart, taking parents from their kids, kids away from their parents. The list goes on and on, Stuart. So no, it's not about what you, or anyone else did to me. As a matter of fact, it's not even about Marcus. It's the principle of the actions at hand leading up to where we're standing right now. The measly fucking donut lickers in this town couldn't give two squirts of piss when it comes to this shit, and not another goddamn soul out here was gonna stand up to you bastards. So, I took matters into my own hands."

"So, what the hell do you want from me then? And what about Diego? He needs to go to a fucking hospital. And put the fucking gun away."

"Stuart, Stu Man, Big Stu, Mayhem... yeah, I really hate to break it to you, bud, but as sure as shit is brown, that is not going to be happening. And I promise you, if you pull out your phone or even so much as try to call for help, I'll end your ass right here in this parking lot too. So, you better think twice about your next moves. Now, we do this my way, or we can do it the hard way. It's up to you."

"Well, what the hell is your way then, huh?"

"You're going to shut the fuck up, go into each one of those cars, get all the phones, money, drugs and weapons, and get your pimply fat ass in the truck. Capiche?"

"Whatever Arabella. I can't believe this fucking shit."

Stuart turned towards the ring of cars and limped towards the first one on the left. As he collected my list of items, I had to go take care of this loose end bleeding out and moaning over on my right.

When I got over to Diego, he was about the same color as the fucking Sunday bulletin. His right eye was dangling on his cheek, and he lay on the ground in the fetal position just gasping for air.

I looked around, I couldn't risk wasting any more bullets and realized the tree line was just a short distance behind where he was, blubbering in a pool of blood, saliva and whatever other bodily fluids I couldn't imagine.

I jogged over to the tree line and almost instantly found a large, jagged rock. It wasn't too heavy that I couldn't manage it on my own, but it sure wasn't a pebble either. The excitement grew in me as I became hungrier with each attack. I made it back to Diego, who still wailed a dull monotonous moan and hadn't so much as moved a muscle since I'd left. I hoisted the boulder as high up in the air as I could withstand and let that thing fall like the goddamn crystal ball in Times Square on New Years Eve.

"Surprise, Bitch" I repeated as a sickening crunch filled the air and brain matter spilled into the already coagulating mess of gelatinous filth.

"Four down, one to go. For now, of course," the devil cheered.

When Stuart finally made it back to Marcus' truck, he had an arm full of necessary supplies. Everything from wads of money sealed with rubber bands, to pocketknives, and more drugs than I'd ever even seen on television. Although I didn't really watch much since Marcus pawned our television for an 8-ball.

"Welcome aboard the fucking Crazy Train. Pleasure having you along for the ride. I'll be your conductor today, do as I say, and this should go over much more smoothly for us both. Please keep your hands, feet and personal belongings inside the vehicle at all times and enjoy the ride."

He nodded with acknowledgement, but his face was plastered with discontent for my little skit.

"Oh, and just for safety's sake...." I began.

POP! POP!

I blew two bullets into his palms that were still face up as he still had an armful of shit.

"That's so you can't just open the door and run off on me."

I quickly tossed the Beretta back under the seat, I noticed he had a Glock right on the top of his pile.

"This will serve me so much better." I thought to myself as I set the gun on my lap.

I reached over, grabbed a handful of pretzels, shoved them all in my mouth at once, and took off towards the road, leaving the second chapter of my legacy in a cloud of dust, just like it began.

Chapter 13
"What a Weird Day"

"For fuck's sake, you crazy bitch, what the hell is wrong with you?"

Stuart's hands were leaking a flood of crimson red mess all over the truck, an improvement I might add, but the upholstery didn't really need more bodily fluids and filth mixed in if I'm being completely honest.

"You're bleeding everywhere, sweetheart. Do you mind? Thing's in mint condition, I'd hate for Marcus to find out you went and got it all a mess."

I chuckled to myself as a minivan approached. The rumble of the muffler could tell you that thing was on its last leg, but by the look of the kayaks strapped on top and bike rack secured on the back, the passengers evidently didn't think so.

"Now what are you gonna do? You're gonna get caught and I swear to god I'm not going down for whatever bullshit you call that back there."

"Ok, so what are *you* gonna do about it?" I retorted. "Because the way it looks to me, you're a big scary guy. You're holding me hostage, with all your dead little friends just a half mile behind us. It doesn't look too good for you."

"I could jump out of this car right now and tell them everything."

"Oh you could, but you won't."

I pulled the S-10 so it would block their path in the road ultimately forcing them to hit us, or stop.

"Now I suggest you go out there and handle this, or you'll find out what lead tastes like for dinner. Sound like a plan Stu Man? You are called Mayhem for a reason, right?"

"Fucking bitch, I oughta end you while I'm at it."

"Now what good would that do you? There're no witnesses, and I'm in the driver's seat. You'll go down for all of it and you know that. The choice is yours though, bud. They're slowing down."

The silver minivan blared its horn three times before coming to a stop and throwing their hazard lights on. It appeared only one woman was in the driver's seat with no other passengers. She rolled her window down and began to yell "What the fuck" but she stopped herself when she saw Stuart climbing out of my passenger side. I guess the bullets didn't stop him as much as I thought they would, but he stayed so I guess that's all that counts.

I stayed in the car. I wanted to watch this unfold, but I also needed a getaway if Stuart didn't keep up his end of the bargain.

He might turn out to be a handy little tool, I pondered. *However, he is a risky investment on my part. Not sure what I'm supposed to do with him alive. I can't just lug him around with me forever.*

I couldn't make out what the two were exchanging, but I knew it was taking longer than I'd hoped.

"He better not be fucking this up."

Not a moment later, the woman's windshield became a stained-glass masterpiece shining in my headlights. I saw Stuart turn back towards me and toss something into the wood line. I'm pretty sure he just slit her fucking neck. That was pretty fucking dope.

What I didn't see coming though, was Stuart pulling a handgun from his waistband and aiming it towards me. Before I could even finish putting the truck in reverse the windshield was shattering around me, sending shards of glass in every direction. Luckily, I was unscathed, just stunned, but damn the view sure was better without a windshield. By some sort of act of only God himself, I managed to throw the truck back into drive and I floored it. I didn't even care if I hit the fucker at this point. I just wanted out of there.

I'm not sure what came first, me yelling "SHIT" or him, but somewhere along the lines, we both did. Next thing I knew, he was up over the hood of the truck and into the bed. Unfortunately for him, he must've landed on some scrap metal that Marcus planned to bring in. I looked in my rearview mirror and Stuart's body was contorted in an extremely unnatural position. A metal fence post erected from his sternum.

"Oof, that had to hurt."

I looked in the mirror one more time to survey the damage I finally received. I mean, it was inevitable. Seven deaths in one day, I was bound to find out eventually. It must have been my lucky day though, because even with a metric fuck ton of glass scattered around me, I managed to only have remnants of my windshield stuck in my hair and one piece hanging from my right eyebrow which funny enough didn't actually hurt yet. I grabbed hold of the shrapnel and gave it a quick yank as blood spurted onto the mirror.

"Goddamn! That hurt…" I winced.

I put the S-10 in drive and carried on down the beaten path. I did not want to be there when the next innocent passerby came through here. And fuck if I wasn't getting tired.

"What a weird fucking day, Arabella." The devil on my shoulder conceded.

"A weird fucking day it was. I'm beat." I huffed.

I brushed the glass off my lap and placed the Glock on the passenger's seat. Hopefully I wouldn't need it again for rest of the night, but better to be safe than sorry.

The last of the sunset had faded to black and, before long, I was pulling down the long, decrepit driveway to the trailer. The lights were still off. Guess Marcus was having a *real* deep sleep, and no visitors had come by to see us either.

What a shame.

Chapter 14
A First for Everything

2 Years Earlier

"Hey babe, what do you want for dinner tonight?"

I was in the kitchen, rifling through the cabinets. I was tired of the same old thing and I wanted to make something new that night for Marcus. He'd been extra sweet lately and I wanted to show my appreciation. I assumed after our little spackle the previous week that he must've felt some remorse and taken into account how he'd been treating me recently. He'd even come home with flowers for me the day before, a mix of sunflowers and roses. It was a gorgeous bouquet.

"How about some chicken, Doll. Chicken actually sounds fucking dope."

"Okay, I'll just run to the store really quick and grab some. Do you want me to grab anything else while I'm out?"

"No, Doll. Take your time though. I'm going to relax."

Strange again, he usually came with me everywhere I went; he didn't like the thought of others looking at me and never trusted me to be anywhere alone.

Maybe he's coming down with something, I thought to myself. I shrugged it off, grabbed the keys, and headed for the door. Big Y was about ten minutes down the street, but they always had better deals than Stop and Shop, which was closer. However, the savings were worth the extra few minutes. Besides, it gave me some much-needed space and alone time.

I got to Big Y and took the extra time Marcus had suggested, perusing the aisles and throwing in a few random things we needed in the house anyway: paper towels, salt, coffee, mayo. Once I got to the poultry cooler, I was pleased to see they had just restocked, I had plenty of options, now it was a matter of deciding what I actually wanted to make. I settled on a package of boneless, skinless chicken breasts. I figured I'd make some lemon pepper grilled chicken with chili lime rice as a side with some steamed broccoli. I grabbed the rest of what I'd need for dinner and headed to the checkout. A pack of Snickers caught my attention, they were Marcus' favorite, maybe

I'd return the gesture and surprise him. Maybe I'd even get lucky if the stars aligned.

The ride back was uneventful. I didn't even hit any red lights, no need for road rage, it was an odd sense of calm. But it felt a little too familiar to the calm before the storm. A notification came across my screen as I pulled into the driveway. I looked down when I parked and was immediately caught off guard.

"Your automatic Verizon payment for $116.82 has been declined, please try again. If the problem persists, please contact your card provider."

I felt my brow furrow as I opened my banking app. I rarely ever needed to do it. We weren't in a tight place where I constantly needed to keep watch on it and our bills were all set to auto-pay. It worked just fine at the store. I couldn't imagine the issue.

My jaw damn near hit the floor when my account balance was not only red, but showed -$2.73.

"What in the FUCK?!?! How did this happen? I just got paid 3 days ago...."

I went to the transactions and my blood began to boil.

Big Y - $84.22

ATM Withdrawal - $200

ATM Withdrawal - $80

ATM Withdrawal - $200

Walmart Purchase with Cashback - $441.88

ATM Withdrawal - $200

Balance Inquiry - $1,203.37

Direct Deposit - $447.59

"Are you fucking kidding me!" I screamed.

I grabbed the bag, and I don't think my feet even hit the ground twice before I made it through the front door. I tossed the bag on the floor and marched into the back bedroom shouting the entire way there.

"Marcus, where is our spare debit card?"

No response...

I repeated myself again a bit louder and with more urgency as I rounded the corner to the bedroom.

"Marcus! Where is our spare debit card?"

I walked in and he instantly jumped tossing something under the bed cover and wiped his left arm as he turned to me.

"Huh? What happened? I don't know what you mean. It should be in my top drawer. What's wrong."

"I don't know Marcus, you tell me... Why is our account in the negative?"

"I don't know, Doll. Did you get paid last week?"

"Yes Marcus, cut the shit. What's with all the ATM withdrawals? Our Verizon payment just got declined and I only spent $85 at the store."

"Ok Arabella, so that's what this is? I do something nice for you for a change and you're going to accuse me of shit? Fuck off. I don't even want your lousy chicken tonight anymore anyways. I'm not hungry."

"No Marcus, that's not *what this is*. I'm not accusing you of shit. I have the proof right in front of me. What the hell did you drain the account for?"

"I didn't drain the account and put it in the negative. You did."

"Fucking pish posh. I spent 85 dollars, Marcus. That never should've sent us into the negatives. Where's the fucking money, and what are you hiding under the blanket?"

"It's nothing," he grumbled with his head low. "I bought some shit off a guy I know, and I was planning on flipping it to double our money. That's all, it's not a big deal. I'll have it all back in the account by the end of the week. Don't worry."

"Bought some *shit*, Marcus? What the fuck's that supposed to mean?"

"Just some shit, Arabella. It's fine, quit bitching about it. I'm going to sleep."

"Whatever, Marcus. You have three days to have that money back in the account or we're done."

I nearly choked on those words as I said them. I'd never threatened him with our relationship before, but this was our livelihood. I could take him having bad days and treating me poorly here and there, but this? This was a line in the sand.

I made sure to put extra emphasis in my stomp as I marched out the door, slamming it behind me. I made my way to the kitchen and began preparing the chicken. I would eat the whole damn meal myself for all I cared. I wasn't letting his bullshit deter me from a good meal.

I'll tell you what, dinner was absolutely phenomenal. One of the best meals I think I've made to date, and it sure as hell tasted even better without the added bitching and gaslighting seasoning the meal. I tossed the few dishes in the sink, knowing I'd finish them later, and threw my coke in the trash. I was surprised Marcus was being so stubborn in his silence. It wasn't like him to not get the last word once the smoke had finally settled.

When I entered the room, I couldn't believe the sight before me, it was like nothing I'd ever even seen before. It took genuine effort not to forget to inhale and exhale each breath. Before me, Marcus sat with his head between his knees, a spoon in one hand, baggies all over the bed, and what appeared to be a needle they give you shots with at the doctor's office lying on the ground. I didn't have the first clue what any of this meant but it looked like a scene straight out of Breaking Bad.

I rushed to Marcus' side and his lips were blue. My stomach sank and a pit the size of a baseball clogged my airway. I fumbled my phone out of my back pocket and immediately dialed 9-1-1.

"9-1-1 What's your emergency?"

"I, I don't know. I just walked into my bedroom and, I don't know, he's not breathing. I think I need an ambulance please hurry!" I managed to stammer out.

"What's the location?"

A few moments went by, and I couldn't process words from sounds and all I could say was

"Help"

"Ma'am what's your location?"

"Uh... uh.... 34 Black Rock Road."

"And what town is that ma'am?"

"P-p-plainville, Plainville ma'am. I'm sorry, please hurry, his lips are blue."

"I have help on the way ma'am. Stay on the phone. Do you know CPR?"

"No, I don't."

Panic began setting in more. Did they really expect me to do CPR and save his life? I didn't even know what to do. What if I hurt him? What if I did it wrong? My heart was racing, and I couldn't even steady my hands, but I put my phone on speaker and set it down beside me.

The dispatcher walked me through the steps and asked me a few other questions. I don't even know if I answered them correctly, or at all to be honest. But I must've done alright because the next thing I knew I was surrounded by what felt like a million different people wearing different uniforms, badges, different medical supplies, and I was being bombarded with a slew of questions.

"What's his name?

"Marcus Raymond Peterson"

"Date of birth?"

"Uh, August 7th, 1992"

"What did he take tonight, Ma'am?"

"I have no clue, we got in a fight, I went to make and eat dinner and I came back and he was blue."

Why does it feel like they are judging me? I thought to myself.

"What's his drug of choice?"

"W-weed. As far as I knew he only smoked weed. But then we got in a fight today over a ton of missing money from my account and he said he bought some 'shit' and I had no idea what he meant until now."

"Okay Ma'am, the medics are working on him. They're going to give him a dose of this spray. It's called Narcan, it should help him wake up so we can bring him to the hospital for medical attention. Do you have a set of shoes for him or anything he'd need to come with us?"

As the medic finished her sentence, I heard Marcus begin to cough and gag and next thing I knew, he was puking goddamn everywhere, showering anyone in a three-foot radius. Like synchronized swimmers, all of the unnecessary personnel that weren't actively working on him all shouted and took a few steps back.

"There she blows!" one of them yelled, but they must not have found him funny because the silent stern glances spoke louder than his poorly placed joke and he quickly put his head back down.

"Well, for all I care, he can go goddamn barefoot and covered in his own filth at this point. And I'll be keeping his phone here too. It's on *my* plan that now wasn't paid for so he won't be needing *that,*" I proclaimed with a sense of bravado that was wildly foreign to me.

"If you say so ma'am. Will you be riding with us, or following the ambulance?"

"Oh no honey, I'm going to get a real night of sleep. Thank you though."

I looked up and a teen boy had unfortunately been given the task of cleaning up the vomit. Poor kid.

The hoard of service workers left my house. The vehicles all proceeded out of the driveway and finally. I was left there in silence. I was hoping for peace, but I wasn't so lucky.

I tore that room apart like a corrections officer who just got word of a shank on the cellblock. I found everything. The needles, I broke them in half and threw them in an empty orange juice container and threw that in the trash.

I flushed the drugs down the toilet. The phone, I factory reset it. Once all was said and done, I was a sweaty, tear-stained mess. I hopped in the shower to wash all the bad of the day away.

When I got out of the shower, feeling a glimmer better than when I'd went in, I had a voicemail on the phone from the hospital. They told me he was stable and asking for me if I wanted to give them a call back or stop in. Otherwise, they'd be transferring him to a nearby rehab facility in the morning. I did not, in fact, give a call or visit.

Two weeks had passed by, and Marcus was begging for me to discharge him and let him come home. He complained that the food wasn't good, his roommate was crazy, and that it was a huge mistake and misunderstanding. He swore he'd never touch anything again, and the first thing he was going to do once he was out of there was propose to me and get me a ring.

I should've known better, but had I known better, we wouldn't be here now. I went and picked him up that night. I wish I could say it was a one and done thing, but that would be a lie.

Chapter 15
BREAKING NEWS

The meltdown was inevitable. It was bound to happen. I wasn't sure when, where, or in what capacity it would come, or how deep, but I knew it was coming. My anxiety was peaking the entire ride home, my knuckles were as white as snow gripping the steering wheel, and each time a car passed me or came up behind me, my heart skipped a couple of beats. The lump in my throat had ceased to disappear, in fact I'm almost certain it actually got worse. My mouth was about the driest it had ever been and the sheer exhaustion of the day setting in was making it immensely harder to keep my eyes open for the short 15-minute drive; but damn was I ever more excited to be home than I was in this moment. I took a second to sit in the driver's seat and recollect the events that had transpired.

A buzzing sound was nagging me from the backseat. I ignored it for a while, but it was incessant. It finally dawned on me; I had 6 cellphones in this vehicle. Mine,

Marcus', David's, Zeke's, Diego's and the other guy's. One of these plug's phones must be going off. Goddamn that was annoying. It's one of those things you don't notice it at first, but once you do, you can't tune it out – like a fly buzzing around, or a clock ticking, or your 10th grade English teacher typing obnoxiously during your entire exam.

I could barely manage to keep my eyes open, but one more buzz and ding from the backseat sent me spiraling. I was wide awake and compelling myself to go through the phones. What would I find? Who knows, but what better did I have to do at this point?

The phones were nothing exciting, honestly. I was stunned however by just how many people were hitting these guys up. Some were absolutely pathetic in their desperate trials to get a response. Others, not so happy to be getting ghosted. Little did they know, they were quite *literally* being ghosted. A few were topless girls that were very clearly strung out looking for a front or a free bag in exchange for their photos, which were nothing to be proud of. Beyond that, there was really nothing to show for, not that I knew what I was really looking for anyhow. Other than that, all that really remained was the group of guys texting each other about meeting David down at the water. They debated back and forth agreeing Marcus needed to be "handled" because he was pulling some slick shit and pretending to be his bitch wanting to go meet up with David for some quicky or some shit.

"Again, little did they know." I giggled to myself, "or didn't, I suppose, considering they're all fucking dead now."

What felt like 30 minutes really turned into hours and hours, and at some point, I must've succumbed to the Sandman. It wasn't until the early morning sunrise was blinding my eyes and my bladder weighed as much as a bowling ball.

What the fuck time was it? I looked at my clock, it was only 6:44. I grabbed the phones, the Glock, and my keys and stumbled to the front door. Once I turned the key and pushed it open, the stench nearly pushed me back out the door.

"Jesus fuck that was unholy levels of putrid." I gagged as a stumbled to the bathroom trying not to pee as I dry heaved the whole way there.

I *needed* more sleep, but that stench was impossible, and the flies were starting to take up residency in the main areas of the house, not just the bedroom. I balled up two cotton balls and shoved them in my nose and meandered to the living room. It had been weeks since either of us had sat on this couch, but it would work for a few hours, there was no way I was going to sleep in that bed. I'd have to figure something out for that, but that is an issue for not 6:45 am Arabella to solve.

I woke up 5 hours later with my face crusted in dry saliva and flies pestering me non-stop. I opened my phone and the first post on my Facebook timeline entirely caught me off guard.

BREAKING NEWS – Killingly, CT
Law enforcement officials in the town of Killingly are seeking the public's help in identifying the suspect of what appears to be a five-person killing spree.

We will keep you updated with more information as it is released, but this is what we know.

Please be advised, there are no known suspects at this moment, and there is no way to know if this was a solo attack or if there are multiple parties involved or if they are armed and dangerous posing a threat to the general population. Please refrain from traveling in the area of the reservoir and remain alert and cautious at all times.

At this time, the victims have been identified as
28-year-old, David Hardman,
31-year-old, Diego Santerre,
19-year-old, Rick Scarborough,
28-year-old, Zeke King,
and 46-year-old Myra Sweeney.
If you have any information regarding this case, Law Enforcement asks that you please call the station or stop in to speak to a detective.

"Oh fuck" I said aloud as I navigated to the comments section.

As expected, it was filled with a bunch of prissy yuppies whining and complaining that the police don't do their jobs and nothing like this ever happens in a small town like ours. Condolences and prayers flooded the log. *That won't help anyone,* I thought to myself with a sinister grin.

"It's about damn time someone cleaned up these streets." – post.

I closed the Facebook app and stretched my arms as far and wide as they would go. I haven't had a sleep that good in I don't even know how long.

Chapter 16
It Was Me

The water swirled around the drain in a cascade of muddled pinks and reds. The water didn't feel like it was washing me no matter how hot I ran it. The pit in my throat had finally relaxed but was replaced by an even larger one in my stomach. My jaw ached from my clenched teeth, my muscles ached, my head was throbbing like a bass drum. I felt trapped within my own body.

This isn't how it was supposed to be.

I tried to close my eyes and let the shower relax me, but flashes of the night before were intruding into every space of my sanity. I kept replaying the news post, the blood spurts, the gunshots; everything was in slow motion.

The gig was almost up, and what for? I didn't feel *any* better.

"Come on Arabella, you're a fucking badass snap out of it" the voice inside my head pleaded.

It wasn't working. I felt like I was drowning. I had to get out of this water. I was becoming claustrophobic, and each drop of water felt like acid rain and ten-pound weights pelting me.

I turned the water off and leapt out of the shower tripping on the shower curtain and pulling the entire rod down with me. My knee caught the edge of the radiator and a stream of blood instantly surfaced and escaped, not helping matters any.

"Son of a bitch!" I yelped.

I grabbed onto the sink and hoisted myself up and quickly wrapped my shirt around my knee to help stop the bleeding. I grabbed my phone off the sink and a force of habit led me to limp into the bedroom to get my clothes, fogging any memory of what lay behind that door.

"Ding" – another phone was going off in the living room, followed by three more.

"Ding"

"Ding"

"Ding"

"SHUT THE FUCK UP" I wailed, out of breath.

The door to the bedroom creaked open and the sound of the flies buzzing around Marcus' body were the first thing that hit me. In that moment, every single thought I could or had been processing went straight out of my brain. I couldn't hear anything beyond a monotonous, deafening buzz.

My breath hitched and quickened; each breath became an independent chore. My hands felt like pins and needles, and I was frozen in my spot in the doorway still naked and holding the blood-stained shirt.

The room around me became a blur, nothing looked how it was supposed to. I felt a rush of power overwhelm me and a sense of strength and urgency I'd never felt before. Marcus's body needed to get the fuck out of this room, and NOW.

Sane and logical thoughts and actions no longer existed as I felt my right hand tighten around the antique lamp by the door and my left hand dropped my phone and the shirt on the ground. I lifted the lamp and yanked the plug out of the wall in one swift motion. I swung the lamp against the wall shattering the top half off sending shards of ceramic flying. All that was left was the bottom of the lamp in my head riddled with jagged pieces poking out of the end. I lifted it above my head and smashed it down over Marcus' face. Because his skin had become such mush it absorbed the blow disgustingly well. Countless broken pieces of ceramic stuck out of his skull and his face looked more like a dart board than a human being.

I pressed one foot to his chest and grabbed onto his arm, I'm not sure why I thought this would work but I leveraged the inner strength of only Hercules himself. I tugged backwards with every ounce of strength in me, and with a quick "Pop" sound I was tumbling backwards into the dresser with Marcus' entire right arm in my hands. I tossed that aside into the hallway and repeated the process with his left.

The left arm came off as well, but not nearly as easily, or clean. The skin on his arm detached first and that's what I went flying with as it degloved from his limb. The arm itself just fell to the side. This was going to be a bigger task than I'd imagined.

Chunks of chocolate pretzels mixed with sour bile ejaculated from my mouth and nose and didn't stop. For at least five minutes I stood there hunched over puking on myself, the floor and everything around me.

Delerium was taking over, I swear to God in those moments I saw Marcus sit up, not the dead Marcus either. He was Marcus from the Stomp, and he had a look of genuine concern on his face. He motioned for me to come sit, patting the clean and made bed beside him.

For a moment, the room was clean, the air was fresh, everything was quiet, and it was just us.

"What's wrong Doll? You look stressed and tired, come rest, what's bothering you?"

I tried to rub my eyes and shake my head, this had to be a dream, but even that didn't help clear the delusions.

"I tried to save you, Marcus. I just wanted *you* back. You gave up on me, you gave up on us! This whole mess with D and Stuart and everyone else, it just got so out of hand. I killed everyone, well except for that one lady, Stuart did that, but I killed everyone, and it didn't bring you back. It didn't take the pain away. I don't have my old life back. I have NOTHING. I can't move on from this, I can't leave this house. What the fuck was I thinking Marcus?"

"You DID save me baby! You saved me from the life I couldn't save myself from. You may not have killed me, that wasn't your fault. But you got all of those monsters off the streets. You did it baby! You just saved so many people being so brave like you were. You're a hero Doll. I'm so proud of you, I would've never been able to do what you did!"

This couldn't be real life. How could I be sitting here, talking to Marcus' ghost?

"Doll, can you do one more favor for me before I go?"

"I don't want you to go Marcus. I want you; I need you. Please, stay."

I was really pleading with an apparition; this was peak insanity. What the fuck was really going on right now. And why the fuck did it feel so real? And why the fuck didn't I want it to end?

"Come take one last hit with me baby. Let's celebrate your win. Please? For me, Doll. You're too beautiful to be this stressed, just take one more hit with me so you can relax, I'll hold you and you can sleep."

"Okay but I have to do one more thing first."

"Okay pretty girl, but hurry, there's not much time left."

I tiptoed over to where my phone lay on the floor and picked it up. I don't know why I felt the need to be so cautious and quiet, but I didn't want to disturb Marcus, He seemed so at peace. I sat back down on the edge of the bed beside him and opened my phone.

"9-1-1 what's your emergency?"

"I'm the one who killed all those guys down at the water, and I'm not sorry. I did what you guys should've done all along and I got the vermin off the street for you. And the death count is actually eight. You're welcome."

"Pardon me, ma'am? Could you repeat that? You're breaking up."

"You heard me just fine." *click*

I placed my phone down beside me and reached behind Marcus' spot in the bed, I knew he had to have something back there. I found a spoon and a fresh needle and a quick glance around the room afforded me with the lighter that had been thrown aside.

I hurried out to the living room and fished through the few things I'd carried in this morning and found the package of wax baggies.

I rushed back to Marcus' side; I couldn't stand the thought of being away from him right now. Although when I returned, the scene was back to reality, I could still hear him talking to me.

This must be the weirdest fucking fever dream. Did I hit my head when I fell out of the shower? Was I imagining this?

The tune of 'Hate Me' by Blue October was playing somewhere in the recesses of my mind as all of this unfolded. It was the same song Marcus used to belt out every time he'd come out of rehab, and it dug deeper and deeper every time. This time, it was strangely comforting.

"Good girl, you know what to do next."

I emptied not one, but two baggies onto the spoon. I couldn't find any water but there was still some blood on the ground that hadn't fully dried.

Again, not thinking clearly, I sucked it up with the syringe and emptied it into the spoon and mixed it around with the powder. I tightened my pink phone cord around my left bicep and made a fist to ensure it was tight enough.

I grasped one of the pieces of the lamp and pulled it from Marcus' face. One arm at a time I sliced from my wrist to my elbow and the blood immediately began to flow.

"*Down the road - not across the street*" I reminded myself.

I had to move quickly, it wouldn't take long for me to lose consciousness, that was only common sense.

I could only hope this would work just as well as all my other plans had, and I could finally relax and be held by my love.

I ignited the lighter beneath the spoon and let it bubble before I sucked the poison into the barrel.

"Good girl Arabella, this will all be over soon, and we can finally relax together."

"I love you, Marcus."

"I love you too, Doll."

I pushed the needle into my arm and emptied the entire 10ml syringe into my vein without leaving a drop.

I curled up into Marcus' cold, stiff arms as best as I could and blinked my eyes as the world became blurry. The sound of the flies vibrated in my ears along with the rhythmic beating of my slowing heart.

I heard 4 dings beside me on my phone and managed to whisper, "It was me," before closing my eyes as everything faded to black.

"Arabella? Are you okay?"

"I saw the Facebook article and then I saw your comment... "

"What's going on?"

"We love you and miss you. Please let us know you're alright."

It was a shame those texts would never be seen.

Epilogue

That same night, Lynn and Marie went down to Marcus and Arabella's trailer. As you can imagine, they were met with the unspeakable. The girls called 911 and the house was flooded once again with emergency personnel. They found everything. The drugs, the guns, the phones; it didn't take long to understand the call made to dispatch earlier that day.

Within days, all the funerals had been planned and held, though not many people showed for any of them. The real action was all behind the screen, people regarding Arabella as a hero for taking down the town's biggest dealers singlehandedly. Others were posting old photos from high school with each of them. Before long, however, everyone that day became a distant memory. Just barstool talk.

No one knows how Arabella mustered up the strength she did to cause so many atrocities, but Lynn and Marie were just thankful she was finally safe.

If you or someone you know is struggling with addiction, abuse, self-harm or anything else PLEASE reach out to someone. Get the help you need and deserve. Don't stay and play a game of what-ifs. Life is too short to spend months on a revenge book as your catharsis. I love you.

Special Thanks

I want to thank Stuart Bray for being one of the most incredible people I've ever had the pleasure of working with. I started out as a reviewer when we first spoke, and I fell in love with his books and writing style. Since then, he has pushed and inspired me to begin, and finish this book. Without him taking me under his wing we would never be here today.

To David Hardy and Timothy King, for also being incredible friends and influences in both my reading and writing journey. You guys have pushed me harder than anyone else to never give up on this book. I owe you both the world.

To my friends and family, who hopefully will never read this book for believing in me blindly and cheering me on along the way.

I owe so much thanks and gratitude to everyone who was along for this ride with me. It was a huge learning experience.

To the people who BETA read for me, thank you, I know I was, and still am a mess, that will never change, thank you for your grace, patience and honesty.

Thank you to my readers. For giving me, and this book a chance. I knew this book was a huge risk, but I wanted to take it on, so if you made it this far, that means I couldn't have messed it up too bad, so thank you, truly. It means more than you'll ever know.

About the author

Laura is a 27-year-old single mom to two incredible boys. She lives in the northeast corner of Connecticut where there is literally nothing to do. She enjoys naps and Snickers more than pretty much anything else. You can often find her reviewing the "bad" books on her TikTok, unless of course that gets banned in this country at the time of publication. Thanks Congress. Her handle is L it.Me.Up. There's really not much else to say, she's really boring.

Made in the USA
Middletown, DE
02 April 2024